VOLLEYBALL VIBE

Karen Spafford-Fitz

D0802310

James Lorimer & Company Ltd., Publishers
Toronto

To Anna and Shannon, my favourite volleyball players.
And to Ken, who delivers the best pep talks ever.

James Lorimer & Company Ltd., Publishers acknowledges funding support from
the Ontario Arts Council (OAC), an agency of the Government of Ontario. We
acknowledge the support of the Canada Council for the Arts, which last year
invested $153 million to bring the arts to Canadians throughout the country. This
project has been made possible in part by the Government of Canada and with the
support of Ontario Creates.

Cover design: Gwen North
Cover image: Shutterstock

9781459415539
eBook also available 9781459415515
Cataloguing data for the hardcover edition is available from Library and Archives Canada.

Library and Archives Canada Cataloguing in Publication (Paperback)

Title: Volleyball vibe / Karen Spafford-Fitz.
Names: Spafford-Fitz, Karen, 1963- author.
Series: Sports stories.
Description: Series statement: Sports stories
Identifiers: Canadiana (print) 2020020954X | Canadiana (ebook) 20200209558 |
ISBN 9781459415508 (softcover) | ISBN 9781459415515 (EPUB)
Classification: LCC PS8637.P33 V65 2020 | DDC jC813/.6—dc23

Published by:
James Lorimer &
Company Ltd., Publishers
117 Peter Street, Suite 304
Toronto, ON, Canada
M5V 0M3
www.lorimer.ca

Distributed in Canada by:
Formac Lorimer Books
5502 Atlantic Street
Halifax, NS, Canada
B3H 1G4

Distributed in the US by:
Lerner Publisher Services
1251 Washington Ave. N.
Minneapolis, MN, USA
55401
www.lernerbooks.com

Printed and bound in Canada.
Manufactured by Marquis in Toronto, Ontario in August 2020.
Job #355198

Contents

1 Zero CHOICE

Bronze Waterfall . . . Autumn Blush . . . Harvest Moon . . . I'm checking out the new fall colours for nail polish. Every one of them is on trend.

I hold my phone close to my face. The coppery tones of Harvest Moon are dazzling. It's definitely my favourite. I'm aching to buy it, but I've spent my allowance already. Who knows when Mom might have the cash to pay me again.

The good news is this is her last year at the University of Alberta. Mom thought she had saved up enough money to finish her program this year. But we learned the hard way that she hadn't. So money has been super tight. It doesn't help that I've never had a dad around to help pay for stuff.

Mom is studying dental hygiene. For some reason, she wants to work inside people's mouths. That's so gross. But at least she'll have some good ideas about the best teeth whiteners to help show off my favourite lip colours.

I'm all caught up on the *Teen Chic* blog. But what about *Posh Gurl Jayne*?

Yes! A new post! "Graphic T-shirt Do's and Don'ts."

I'm reading it when Mom bursts through the door. She's carrying a stack of binders. Her hair, as usual, is a wreck. I suggested some oil products and a flat-iron to control the frizz. But Mom just gave me a killer glare, so I guess that's out.

"Can you shut that door behind me, Ria?" Mom asks.

"Sure," I say. My eyes are still fixed on the cute cropped T-shirt with the little pineapple on it.

I look up from my screen and see Mom pointing at the oven.

"What about the salmon?" she says. "I asked you to put it in the oven at five o'clock."

"Oops. I got busy and forgot."

Mom runs her hand through her hair, which does nothing to tame the frizz. "Busy doing what?"

I hold up my phone. "Doing some reading," I say. "You'd really like these T-shirts because —"

Mom cuts me off. "I have zero interest in those T-shirts. Or in anything else you've been reading on your phone for the past two hours about fashion and makeup."

Her mouth is a straight, tight line. I can tell this isn't the right time to mention that her lack of interest in fashion really shows. Her baggy T-shirt and blue jeans aren't helping her overall look at all.

Mom plants her hands on her hips. "Ria," she says, "all this time online needs to stop. Do you even remember when you used to read books?"

"Sure," I say. "I started reading that library book you got me. It was about those two kids. They were going on a trip. But then I got distracted and —"

"— and you never picked it up again," Mom says. "Last year, you spent all your time after school either on your phone or at the mall. I knew junior high was new for you and I wanted to give you some time to pull it together. But it's a week into grade eight and you still aren't making good use of your time. You're hardly interacting with anyone at all. So I'm giving you a choice."

Oh no! Whenever an adult says 'I'm giving you a choice,' it really means you have zero choice. It means they have already chosen for you.

"You will do one of two things," Mom continues. "You will either get a job, or you will play on a school team. Since I'm not around after school, I need to know you're doing something worthwhile."

Heat spreads across my whole face. *Stay calm, Ria! Think!*

"A job sounds interesting," I nod. I'm trying to show her I'm serious about my supposed choice. "But you have to be eighteen to be a beauty advisor at Sephora."

"That might be true," Mom says. "But you can get a babysitting job when you're much younger. And your aunt needs some help after school."

"Eww, Mom! You're kidding me, right?"

"I'm not kidding you. Aunt Kana just took another toddler into her day home. Along with the babies, her hands are full. By the end of the day —"

"By the end of the day," I finish for her, "she needs help dealing with their runny noses and nasty diapers."

Just thinking about the crying, germy little kids Aunt Kana babysits makes me cringe. Any time I even walk near a baby or a toddler, they start to cry. I can't deal with those scenes. But Mom thinks I could become a babysitter? Not a chance!

"I mean, good for Aunt Kana," I say. "But I am so not the person for that job."

"Okay," Mom says. "Then you'll be joining a school team. So what sport will it be?"

"I don't know," I say. "I haven't paid much attention to the school announcements."

"Of course, you haven't," Mom sighs. "That's because you've been too focussed on your phone — even while you're at school."

"True," I say. "But school doesn't officially start until after the morning announcements."

"I'm not going to debate that with you," Mom says. "My point is this: you need to get onto whatever team is starting up. I don't care what team that is. And since I don't have classes tomorrow afternoon, I can meet you at the school office to ask about it."

"Mom — *no!*" A block of ice is forming in the pit of my stomach.

Mom peers straight into my face. "Then you had better get this done, Ria. I'm going to text you tomorrow at noon. And if you don't have any answers about which school team you've chosen, I'll be there to talk to your principal."

I throw my hands into the air. "Okay," I say. "I can't believe this is all because I forgot to put some salmon into the oven!"

Mom gives one more sigh, then storms upstairs. Everything about this feels wrong. Like, I'm the teenager here. Isn't it supposed to be *me* having a fit?

As for this school-team thing, it's a lot to wrap my head around. I'm not bad at gym class. But I'm not exactly the sporty type, either. I've never been on an actual team in my whole life.

It looks like that's about to change.

2 TRYOUT

This morning, Mom was still talking about me joining a team. She made me take extra gym clothes to school. She still had that same mean glint in her eye from last night.

When the morning announcements start, I'm staring at my phone. I have it angled inside my desk. I stop reading about "The New Fall Wardrobe" to listen.

"A final reminder that after school today, Mr. Omar will meet with all girls in grades eight and nine who are interested in trying out for the senior girls' volleyball team."

I don't know if 'interested' is the right word.

"Be in the gym, dressed and ready to play, at 3:45."

Minutes later, the announcements end with a click.

I asked around this morning. The only other team is cross-country running. They've already been training. Plus, I can't see myself just running — and sweating. So, I guess my new sport will be volleyball.

I text Mom.

Volleyball tryout after school.

Apparently, I'm not the only one in the family who reads her phone during class. Exactly one second later, Mom replies.

Great! Have fun!

Fun? Good one, Mom!

All day long, I can't stop thinking about losing my free time. And how will I look out there on the volleyball court? I'll be as awkward as a baby giraffe on skates — while everyone watches and judges. My stomach quivers.

When my last class ends, I fix my hair and makeup at my locker. I also do some deep breathing to try to calm myself.

I'm ten minutes late getting to the gym. That works well because some other girls are setting up the net. Mr. Omar is standing nearby with a clipboard in his hand. He's a new teacher at Yana Malko Junior High.

Meanwhile, Sutton is directing the other girls on how high the net has to be. I should have known she would be here. Our moms were on the parent council together when we were in elementary school. Sutton was into volleyball even then. I remember her parents hired a personal trainer for her. If my mom had that kind of money to spend on me, I would have gone for a personal stylist instead. Then again, Sutton doesn't seem to be sweating this volleyball thing like I am. The tryout hasn't even started yet and actual sweat is trickling inside my T-shirt. Yuck!

Mr. Omar steps into the middle of the gym and blows a whistle. I take another deep breath and join the others.

"Thanks, everyone, for meeting today," he says. "Before we start, I'd better check names. I don't think everyone signed up on the list outside the office."

I definitely didn't sign up. Maybe this is my way out!

"Zina, Iris, Alya, Monzi . . ." The girls raise their hands when Mr. Omar says their names.

Sutton, of course, shoots her whole arm up when he gets to her. "I'm here!"

Oh, god. The kissing-up starts! I think.

"Whose name didn't I call?"

I slowly raise my hand.

"Your name is?" he asks.

"Ria Tanaka," I say.

Two other girls, Chen and Olivia, also give him their names. While he writes them down, I think about not trying too hard. If I don't make the team, Mom might feel really bad for me. Maybe she won't force me into diaper duty at Aunt Kana's day home after all.

Mr. Omar looks up from his list. "I just counted," he says. "We have twelve people. That's the number I planned to bring onto the team. That will give us two full lines for playing games during practice.

"So," he says, "the tryout is officially over. Congratulations! You've all made the team!"

What? That happened way too fast!

A shriek echoes throughout the gym.

"Yes! I love it!" Sutton is jumping up and down.

Meanwhile, Iris and Alya are rolling their eyes. The three of us definitely agree about Sutton. I'm not exactly friends with Iris and Alya, but I went to the mall with them a few times last year. I hardly had any money to spend. That's maybe why they stopped asking me. After that, I just went by myself. In some ways, that was easier anyway.

"The volleyball season starts soon," Mr. Omar says. "So it's great that tryouts are over. We have a lot to do before our first match.

"First of all," he continues, "we need to choose a team captain. This is the person you can go to if you have a problem. It's also someone who will be a leader on the court. If anyone would like to nominate another teammate —"

"I'd love to be team captain!" Sutton says.

"Didn't you hear the part about 'nominating another teammate'?" Alya asks.

Sutton slumps over. She turns her sad, puppy-dog eyes to the tile floor.

"How about this," Mr. Omar offers. "Talk to me after practice if you'd like to nominate another teammate or volunteer for the position. I'll decide and let everyone know tomorrow.

"But first," he says, "we have some work to do today."

Something about the way Mr. Omar says that makes me sweat even harder.

What did I just get myself into?

3 Feeling the BURN

Mr. Omar rolls over a basket filled with volleyballs. "I'd like six Ravens on each side of the court."

Ravens? What's he talking about?

I'm looking around me for a clue. Then the massive raven painted on the gym wall catches my eye. Its wings are spread as though it's flying. The words 'Malko Ravens' are painted above it.

I guess that answers my question. That's the name for the teams at Yana Malko Junior High. Somehow, I just became a Raven. It's not the team name I'd have chosen, but whatever.

I shuffle to the other side of the court with five other girls.

"We'll start with some serving," Mr. Omar says.

Sutton's hand flies into the air. "Do you want overhand or underhand serves?" she asks.

I swallow hard. Do these girls actually do overhand serves? Whenever I've seen people doing them, they've looked super hard.

Feeling the Burn

"Your choice," Mr. Omar says.

As I'm walking to the back of the court, I try to remember the volleyball rules I learned in gym class. I know that someone serves the volleyball. Then, the other team can pass the ball around to each other. But the third time they touch it, they have to hit the ball back over the net.

Sutton, Iris and Alya are hammering balls over with hard overhand serves. So are Chen, Saige and Monzi. As for me, I'll stick to underhand.

"Let's see your serve, Ria," Mr. Omar says.

Oh man! It starts! I think.

I cup the ball in my right hand. I draw my left fist back, pop the ball into the air, and swing through.

Yes! It's going over the net!

But — oh no! It just hit the ceiling!

My face burns. I keep my eyes down. I don't want to know who saw my crappy serve.

"Not good, right?" I say.

"If this was a game," Mr. Omar says, "the other team would get a point. But your serving weight was good. You just swung through too far. You need to stop before your hand is pointing at the ceiling or that's where the ball will go."

Mr. Omar moves on. Meanwhile, balls are flying everywhere. I dodge a cannonball that nearly hits me in the face. Some of my underhand serves make it over the net. But most of them hit the roof or fly sideways.

Mr. Omar blows the whistle. "We'll practise the forearm pass next. It's also called 'bumping' the ball, or 'passing' it. Who can help me demonstrate?"

Sutton, of course, is waving her arms.

"Thanks, Sutton," Mr. Omar says. "In a minute, I'll have you toss that ball toward me. But first, I want to show everyone the ready position." He bends his knees and holds both hands in front of him. "Notice that while I'm bending down, my weight is on my toes. That's so I can move fast and get to the ball."

He stays in the ready position. "Okay, Sutton," he says. "Toss me the ball."

Mr. Omar rushes to it. Then he brings his arms together and hits the ball with his wrists.

"Get into partners," Mr. Omar says. "Start practising your forearm passes."

Partners. That's awkward. None of these girls are really my friends. And most of them already have someone to work with.

"Do you have a partner?" I turn around. A tall girl with dark braids is talking to me. I think she's new at Yana Malko.

"Not yet," I say. "Do you want to do this passing thing?"

"Sure," she smiles. "I'm Zina, by the way."

"Hey. I'm Ria."

We start passing the ball back and forth. Most of

Zina's passes come straight to me. But mine are flying off in random directions. Plus, my arms hurt from all this passing. My legs ache from crouching in the ready position.

Mr. Omar blows the whistle minutes later. "Drop the volleyballs back into the basket," he says.

Oh, thank god we're done!

"We're going to move on to some conditioning," Mr. Omar says.

What? There's more?

"Find a spot on the wall," he says. "Time to start your first wall sit. Your knees should be bent at a ninety-degree angle."

Oh no! Ms. Zafar sometimes makes us do those in gym class. They're brutal!

"Twenty more seconds!" Mr. Omar calls.

My legs are burning and shaking.

"Ten, nine, eight . . ." Mr. Omar counts down.

I stand up.

Mr. Omar stops and stares at me. "We'll all try that again," he says.

The other girls groan. They're looking at me with murder in their eyes. Mr. Omar is starting back at the beginning. So there's another full minute of this torture — and my legs are already trashed!

After that, Mr. Omar makes us do push-ups and sit-ups. Next, we do those plank things where you hold yourself up between your forearms and your toes.

"Keep your bodies straight," Mr. Omar calls. "No sagging."

By the time we've finished, I'm ready to puke. Whoever invented planks should be thrown in jail.

"That's it for today," Mr. Omar says. "I'll post our schedule on the school website. Next practice is tomorrow after school. Games start this week, too. We're going to have a great volleyball season."

Somehow, I'm not so sure about that last part.

As I leave, my legs feel like licorice sticks. I think back to the "choice" Mom gave me to babysit or play on a team. I still think joining the team was the right choice. But I might change my mind.

4 Pass, Set, HIT!

Last night, I looked up some volleyball rules online. So now I know not to hit the ball out of bounds. And not to touch a ball the other team fires out of bounds, even if it's on our side of the net.

I was starting to read about the different positions when I fell asleep. I didn't even get to read the latest *Teen Chic* post.

"Ria!" Mom calls. "You're late!"

"What?" I grab my phone and check the time.

It's 7:55? Oh no!

I jump out of bed. My legs are so shaky I nearly collapse on the floor. And it feels like all my internal organs got crunched together. But it gets worse, because I have to leave the house by 8:20. So I either have to skip breakfast or skip flat ironing my hair.

The choice is obvious. I stagger into the bathroom and reach for my flat iron. But my arms hurt so much I can't hold them up for more than a few seconds at a time.

I settle for straightening just my bangs. Then I pull the rest of my hair into a cute, messy bun. Even that is painful. Plus, I'm starving. I stumble downstairs.

"Here," Mom says. She hands me two muffins in a plastic baggy. "I thought you might need these." She also hands me my lunch from the fridge.

I hurry out the door as fast as my throbbing legs can carry me. I grit my teeth as I climb up into the bus.

Over the course of the day, my muscles loosen up a bit. Still, I'm dreading practice. It wouldn't be so bad if we just did volleyball stuff. But Mr. Omar's idea of conditioning is seriously twisted.

After school, Mr. Omar calls us into the middle of the gym.

"Our first match is tomorrow," he says. "The volleyball season always starts earlier than we can fully prepare for. But that will be the same for the Scorpions, too.

"And for this season," he adds, "Sutton will be our team captain."

Sutton is jumping up and down. Now, she's pumping her fists into the air. I don't know why she's acting so surprised. After all, she nominated herself.

"If anyone needs to speak with Sutton privately about anything," Mr. Omar continues, "please feel free to do so."

Sutton is bobbing her head the whole time.

"Let's start with some basics," Mr. Omar says. "At

each of our matches, the team that wins two out of three games is the winner. The first two games go to 25 points. You have to win each game by at least two points. That means some games could go even higher than 25. If each team has won one game, we'll play a third game as a tie-breaker. And that game only goes to 15."

Iris and Alya are doing their most bored expressions.

"Does this guy ever stop talking?" Iris mutters.

"No kidding," Alya says. "We know this stuff already."

Really? It's all new to me. But I nod and try to look like I knew it, too.

"During games," Mr. Omar continues, "each team gets three touches on the ball. The first touch is the forearm passing we did yesterday. The second touch is an overhand pass. It's also called a volley, or a set. The third touch is when we attack and send the ball back over the net. We sometimes switch it up to surprise the other team. But for the most part, those are the three touches on the ball. Pass, set, hit."

Iris and Alya are still looking bored, like this is the most obvious thing on Earth.

"Pair up, and we'll practise some volleying," says Mr. Omar.

I take a look around. Zina is working with Meg. As for the others —

"Ria! Over here!" The shriek carries across the gym. "I have a ball!" Sutton holds it up.

I can see that, Sutton! I think.

Sutton tosses me the ball. I volley it back to her in an overhand pass. I think I'm doing okay. But Sutton doesn't seem to think so.

"Get your hands up by the sides of your forehead," she says. "Imagine they're reindeer antlers."

Reindeer antlers? Really? Are we in grade one?

Still, I try what she says. And it works. My reindeer-antler volley sends the ball upward in an arc.

"You got it!" Sutton squeals.

Everyone looks at me. My face burns. But at least I'm doing better. We volley back and forth until Mr. Omar stops us.

"We'll move on to hitting now," he says. "Everyone, line up near the net. When I set the ball to you, I want to see a big approach. Run hard toward it. Then jump up and do a full arm swing."

On their turns, Iris and Alya slam the ball. It looks like the other girls have done this before, too. And now I'm up!

My heart is thumping as Mr. Omar volleys the ball to me. When it's in the air, I run forward. I jump, like he said to. But I've already landed before I can reach the ball. My hit slams into the net.

"Your timing is a bit off, Ria," Mr. Omar says. "But you'll get there."

We do this about a million times before Mr. Omar lets us stop.

Pass, Set, Hit!

"We have time for a short game," he says. He divides us into two teams, and I go to my spot on the court.

When the game starts, I feel like I'm mostly pivoting in tight little circles, hoping the ball doesn't come to me. When it does, I hit it away from me as fast as I can. My head is swimming even more when Mr. Omar starts talking about the different positions. Setter, hitter and blocker.

It turns out Sutton has already played as setter. So she's going to take that position again. She's the person we're supposed to pass the ball to when it comes over the net. Then she'll volley it over to the hitters.

Mr. Omar asks Saige, Zina and Eve to be blockers. Their job is to block the ball at the net to stop the other team from hitting it over to us. Everyone else will be hitters.

"I'm looking for another setter," Mr. Omar says. "We need two on the court all the time. Who else wants to try that position?"

No one speaks up. I don't know why setting is such a big deal. Still, there's no way I'm going to volunteer.

Mr. Omar frowns. "I'll talk to some people privately about being a setter. But for today, we need to wrap up. The match starts tomorrow at four o'clock. We'll warm up at three-thirty. You'll have to hustle here after your last class."

Sutton raises her hand. "I'd like to finish with the team cheer," she says.

Um, what?

"Everyone," Sutton says, "put one fist down into the middle."

We have to wait for Iris and Alya to join us.

"I need to hear 'Ravens' after one," Sutton says. "Three, two, one —"

"Ravens!" Everyone yells the team name together. At the same time, we throw our fists into the air.

Okay, that's kind of cute. But what's not cute is how my knees are shaking as I pull on my hoodie. I'm one of the last to leave, behind Iris and Alya.

"This team totally sucks," Iris mutters.

"I know," Alya says. "I can't believe Mr. Omar picked Sutton for captain over you."

They look back at me. I guess Alya must have nominated Iris for team captain. I don't know what to say. I might have an idea why Mr. Omar didn't pick Iris. But I'm not going to say a word!

I shoot Iris a sympathetic look. Then I hurry out of the school.

5 Malko RAVENS

"I'm sorry I'll miss your first match," Mom says.

"How did you . . .?"

I hadn't told Mom about the match. She's so into her courses that I can't trust her out around actual people. I never know when Mom will start talking about weird things. Like how her whole class practised freezing people's mouths by shoving needles into chicken breasts. She gave way too much information about how chicken breasts have almost the same texture as the inside of people's mouths. So gross! I don't think I was the only person in the meat section of the supermarket who nearly puked that day.

Mom interrupts my thoughts. "I heard about the match from Jessica Steen," she says.

"Who's that?" I ask.

"That's Sutton's mom. I bumped into her at Sobey's yesterday."

I'm on high alert. I don't think anything good can

come of my mom and Sutton's mom talking — even if they're just grocery shopping.

"It's okay that you'll miss it," I say. "It's our first match, so we'll suck anyway."

"Everyone has to play their first match at some point," Mom says. "You need to go in with a positive attitude."

I'm trying to figure out how to reply to that when Mom sticks it to me.

"Jessica is picking up Sutton after the practices and games. She offered to drive you home, too."

What? That's not good.

Sutton makes me cringe every time I'm near her. Driving home with her doesn't work for me. Plus, I still want to fit in a trip to the mall. Mr. Omar has to give us a day off soon.

"Actually," I say, "I don't mind riding the bus."

It's hard to choke out those words. Because actually, I hate riding the bus. It's crowded. It smells. Sometimes, people even try to talk to me — even though I wear earphones. When I was in elementary school, I just had to walk across the street to get there. But to get to my junior high, I have to take the city bus.

"It'll start getting dark sooner in the next few weeks," Mom says.

"Maybe I can catch a lift with Sutton's mom then." I use a breezy tone. With any luck, Mom will let this idea go.

"I worry about you," Mom says, "with the bus letting you off at the plaza. Then you having to walk home from there by yourself. And you know," she continues, "Sutton has done a lot of volleyball clinics. She might have some tips to help you out."

Oh god! I can imagine Sutton talking my ear off while she shares her volleyball wisdom with me. My jaw clenches. At this rate, I'll need Mom to fit me with one of those ugly tooth guards so I don't grind my teeth down to the bone!

"I already told Jessica you'd be happy to ride home with her and Sutton," Mom says. "It was a lovely offer for her to make."

I'm about to argue. But something about the set of Mom's mouth tells me it would be pointless. Like it or not, Sutton has become my new travel buddy.

★ ★ ★

After school, I spend some extra time on my fresh-faced, natural makeup look. That actually takes more time than the name suggests. If I have to wear that tragic team jersey with the black bird on the front, my makeup needs to be spot on. I also use lots of hairspray to keep my ponytail in place. I'm the last one into the gym.

I brush past the teachers, students and parents on the side benches. They're laughing and calling out to each other. My stomach is twisting into a hard knot. Couldn't they go someplace else?

"Hurry up, Ria!" Mr. Omar calls. "You're late!"

I drop my backpack by our team bench. My ugly Malko Ravens jersey burns against my skin as I join the team on the court. Everyone is warming up by practising their serves. Hopefully, this will keep my mind off puking.

I finally see a ball coming straight to me. I'm running for it when Alya zips in. She scoops up the ball. I skid to a stop so I don't bump into her. Her perfect overhand serve goes deep into the other side of the court. Then she turns and notices me.

"What?" she asks.

I want to tell her that was actually my ball.

Not a good idea, Ria! I tell myself.

"Nice serve," I say.

Before I can touch a single ball, Mr. Omar calls us over to practise hitting. Everyone is lining up. Mr. Omar tosses the volleyball into the air, then hits it downward. The player at the front of the line has to hurry to the ball, then do a forearm pass.

The line is moving fast. The knot in my stomach is tightening again. When it's my turn, my teeth rattle as I connect with the ball. But at least I return it. Next, we practise hitting at the net. We've just finished when the Scorpions arrive.

We move off the court while they do their serving

warm-ups. Still, my eyes are glued to the court. Their serves are as hard as the ones Sutton, Iris and Alya do.

I'm in so much trouble.

"Remember to use all three hits on the ball," Mr. Omar says. "Pass, set, then hit into their zone. We need to get some attacks going. Like I told you yesterday, Sutton is our first setter. Eve has also agreed to play as setter today. So when the first ball comes over the net, pass up to Sutton or Eve — whoever has rotated into the front row."

He says some other things, too. But now the two line judges are stepping onto opposite corners of the court with flags in their hands. The blood is pulsing hard in my temples.

Sutton nudges me, and I tune back in.

"Everyone will get a chance to play today," Mr. Omar says. "Our starting line-up is Sutton, Zina, Ria, Eve, Iris and Alya." He reads our names from a slip of paper.

Oh no! Why is Mr. Omar putting me out to play already? I wanted to watch at least one game first!

He hands the paper to Sutton. "Run that over to the scorekeepers," he says.

The noise level in the gym is rising. My nerves are totally shot. At first, I can't figure out why I'm so panicky, but then it hits me. The same way I need my hair and my makeup to look polished, I also need to look cool. Like I know what I'm doing. But that's not going to happen. Maybe I should have thought more about working for Aunt Kana. Maybe I could have found a way to avoid the smelly diapers.

The ref blows her whistle. "Team captains?" She motions the two girls to centre court. Sutton and the captain for the Scorpions shake hands. The ref tosses a coin into the air.

"Heads," Scorpion Girl calls out. A moment later, the coin lands on the gym floor.

"It's tails," the ref says.

"We'll take first serve," Sutton says, then she bounces back to us.

Time to get this over with, I say to myself.

I'm walking onto the court when Sutton pulls me back. "You have to wait for the ref to blow the whistle!"

I think Sutton is trying to whisper. But she has the loudest "whisper" known to mankind. And now everyone is looking at me. They know I've already messed up — and the game hasn't even started yet!

"Plus, we need to do the team cheer," Sutton continues. "So, three, two, one —"

"Ravens!" we call out.

My voice cracks on the team cheer. But somehow, I think that's the least of my worries.

6 GAME ON!

The ref blows the whistle. Sutton delivers a hard over-hand serve. It sails over the net and deep into the back row.

The Scorpions seem thrown off by how fast Sutton's serve came at them. Their player gets under the ball, but her pass doesn't make it all the way to the setter.

"Help!" the setter calls.

The Scorpions player nearest the ball sets it up. A hitter takes a run at it. Then time does a funny wobble. I hardly have a chance to see the ball before it slams onto the gym floor beside me. The Scorpions are cheering hard as the ref signals it's their point.

"Ria! That was your ball!" Alya calls.

"Move your feet!" Iris yells.

I shrink. All the blood in my body is rushing toward my burning-hot face. The Scorpions got the first point because of me. Now they get to serve, too.

It feels like the Scorpions are targeting me. Because their server sends the ball straight to me again.

"Mine!" I try to sound confident. But I send the ball right to the blocker on the other side. She reaches up and tips it over the net. I wasn't ready to touch the ball again so soon. Sutton and Zina are racing over to help, just as the ball lands at my feet.

The Scorpions go wild at taking the first two points.

Now that we're down, the Scorpions score point after point. They get us on out-of-bounds plays, on serves that smack the ceiling, on hits that land in the net.

Somewhere in there, I get one pass to Sutton. And later, when Eve can't get to the ball in time to set it, I manage a decent set for her.

Still, the Scorpions are going hard. It's 18–7 for them. They're finishing us off fast.

Mr. Omar is calling out to us. "Be ready out there," and "Good try, girls!" But nothing is helping.

I look over to see Mr. Omar standing at the side with Olivia. He's signalling something to the ref by rolling his hands.

"Substitution," he says. "Number eleven in for number seven."

Number seven. That's me.

Olivia high-fives me as I step off the court. While I plunk down on the bench, I feel like I can finally breathe again. It's safer here — especially when the Scorpions get a string of serves going. This also gives me a chance to take in the game. Somehow, my eyes keep landing on Sutton.

She's super focused and she's directing everyone around her on the court. She totally knows what she's doing out there. Wow.

And now, something else is going on. With each play, my pulse is rising and falling with the action. I imagine myself out there on the court. But this time, I see myself actually helping my team. I'm hoping that might be possible.

Mr. Omar has made more substitutions. Now Iris is sitting beside me on the bench. Her arms are crossed. Whenever the Scorpions get a point, she mutters and shakes her head. The excitement I was feeling is taking a nosedive. I feel completely flat and lifeless. And now we're down 24–14.

Mr. Omar substitutes more players. But we can't turn the game around. When the Scorpions score their final point, the Ravens shuffle over to the bench.

"Not exactly the start we wanted," Mr. Omar says. "But we'll try to take the next two games."

Iris lets out a deep sigh.

Alya is standing partly behind Mr. Omar. She mouths two words to the group. "As if."

Mr. Omar continues. "Those who didn't start in the first game will be on the court next. Sutton and Eve will be setting again."

We change ends for game two. The ref blows the whistle. The new lines step onto the court.

"Okay, girls," Mr. Omar says. "Let's see lots of energy out there!"

Their server sends a hard ball over. Faye passes the ball to position two for Eve to set. Meg hits it toward the end of their court.

"It's out!" The Scorpions player nearest the ball holds her hands back. She isn't touching it.

The ball hits the floor close to the line. The line judge crouches down to see exactly where it touched the floor.

"Out." He raises the flag into the air.

"Yes!" The Scorpions are all cheering.

The next serve comes hard. Eve and Faye get tangled up in the middle of the court. Neither girl gets a pass away.

"Would you call the ball out there!" Iris waves her arms as she yells.

Mr. Omar turns to Iris. "It's important to stay positive," he says. "We only encourage our teammates — ever!"

Faye picks up the next serve. She passes to Sutton in the front row.

"Mine!" Sutton yells.

"Over here!" Meg calls.

Sutton sets it to her, and Meg slams it over the net.

It seems like that play changes the game.

"Come on, Ravens! You've got this!" Everyone is cheering hard. I'm caught up in the excitement, too — yelling along with the others.

Faye and Monzi do some big hits over the net. The score is 18–16 for us.

"Time out!" the Scorpions coach calls.

Our players bounce over to the bench. Everyone crowds around them.

"Good job out there," Mr. Omar says. "But it's not time to celebrate yet. We still have more work to do! If we can keep our hits in the court, we can take this game. We can force the third game."

The ref blows the whistle to end the time out. The players return to the court.

"Come on, you guys!" we yell from the bench. I'm surprised how much I'm getting into this game!

The Ravens and the Scorpions each get one point. But now, two of the tallest girls on the Scorpions are blocking us at the net. We can't get any hits past them.

The momentum completely shifts. Soon, it's 24–19 for the Scorpions. I can't believe how fast that happened.

"Game point!" the ref calls.

The whistle blows. The Scorpions server sends over a fast, hard ball. But it's low. As it hits the top of the net, I'm holding my breath.

"Over! Over!" they're all shouting.

And it does go over. Sutton and Saige try to play the ball, but it's wobbling down along the net. They can't get under it — and it falls to the floor.

Scorpions, 25. Ravens, 19. So much for us forcing that third game. We lost the match in two straight games!

I wonder if our whole season is going to be like this.

7 Team TROUBLE

My whole body feels heavy here on the bench. I didn't exactly choose to be on this team. But losing two straight games in my first match wasn't my number-one choice, either.

"Time to go shake hands," Mr. Omar says.

I take a deep breath, then I haul myself to my feet. Sutton goes first as our team files past the Scorpions by the net.

"Good game. Good game," everyone says as we go down the line.

The gym is emptying out as we join Mr. Omar at the bench.

"That was a solid first effort," he says. "Now everyone has a feel for playing in an actual game. And we came close to forcing a tie-breaker. We have more matches next week," he continues. "Monday's practice is going to be pretty intense."

Oh god! My muscles are burning at the thought!

"I'll turn things over to your team captain," Mr.

Omar says. "Sutton, do you have any thoughts to share?"

"I do," she says.

Surprise, surprise!

"I think the Scorpions beat us because we got down on ourselves. Especially when their blockers stopped our hits. Also," she adds, "we need to remember what we learned at our volleyball camps and clinics. If anyone has worked with personal trainers, it would be good to check in with them, too."

Volleyball camps and clinics? Personal trainers? Am I the only one who can't afford those?

I'm shuffling out the door when Iris and Alya slide in beside me.

"That totally sucked," Iris says. "I don't know why Mr. Omar didn't substitute more players."

"Yeah," Alya mutters. "Hardly anybody could even hit the ball over."

"No kidding," Iris says. "And we didn't lose because we were 'getting down on ourselves.' Sutton doesn't know what she's talking about."

"Oh, do you mean our team captain?" Alya laughs.

"Exactly," Iris says. "She's a total joke."

Iris and Alya look at me. I think they're waiting for me to agree with them. But I don't know what to say.

Sure, our team lost. I don't like that either. But I thought Sutton knew what she was doing out there. I remember how the excitement in the gym was electric during the games. That feeling is turning more and more sour with every word they say.

Then I realize something else. After what they said about Sutton, I don't want them to see me getting in her mom's van with her.

"Hey, Ria," Iris says, "maybe we could hang out at the mall sometime."

The mall. My heart usually flutters at the thought of my favourite stores. Sephora. Aritzia. Even the nail polish section at London Drugs. But today, too many other things are running through my head.

Alya and Iris are still looking at me. I spot a water fountain up ahead.

"I've got to stop here," I say. I take the longest drink in history.

By the time I stand up, Alya and Iris have moved on. Thank goodness for that. The whole conversation with them finished me off. Every muscle in my body feels fried as I step outside.

"Ria!" Sutton screeches out my name.

I glance around. At least Iris and Alya have gone. I give Sutton a wave, then I climb into the van.

Like I thought, Sutton talks non-stop the whole way home. She blats out every little detail of the match to her mom. How does she remember all those plays?

But I'm starting to understand what Sutton is talking about. I'm learning some stuff from her — even though part of me wants her to be quiet already.

Jessica clears her throat. She maybe realizes Sutton has done all the talking. "What did you think of the match, Ria?"

"It was okay," I say. "It's all pretty new to me."

"Well, it is your first game," Jessica says. "So that's bound to be the case."

Sutton speaks up again. "Ria, I could help you."

She doesn't pause to see if I even want her help.

"Like, with your serve," she says. "We could work on that. Because it's too easy for the other team to return your serve."

Really? I didn't think my serve was that bad. I get the ball over the net most of the time.

"Your hits could use some work, too," Sutton continues. "And you're not so very short. But you're not really tall, either."

My thoughts turn to Mom. Her parents were Japanese. Maybe that's why she's so short. I don't know anything about my dad. But I'm already taller than Mom is.

"This is maybe as tall as I'm going to get," I say.

"I know some good drills for working on your vertical," Sutton says. "That'll make up for height. We could practise them together."

Sutton looks at me like she's waiting for an answer. But I don't know what to say. I don't really want to spend more time doing extra volleyball work. With

Mr. Omar's practices and lots of games coming up, that already seems like enough. Maybe it's even more than enough.

I'm about to tell Sutton 'no thanks.' Then I stop myself. I actually could use some help.

We're pulling up to my place and I still can't decide how to handle this. So I don't exactly answer Sutton.

"Thanks for the ride, Jessica," I say. Then I shoot out of the car as fast as my aching legs will carry me.

"Meet you at the school park tomorrow!" Sutton shrieks. "At eleven o'clock."

8 At the PARK

I do a long, slow stretch across my bed. It's finally Saturday. I've never needed a weekend so badly. I roll over and pick up my phone. 10:43.

Ever since Alya and Iris mentioned the mall, I've been wondering about Sephora's new products. I'm scrolling through their website when voices drift upstairs. Mom has to study for an exam. I'm sure she'll get rid of whoever is at the door.

I turn back to the Sephora website. Just then, another voice — loud and shrill — rings out.

"What? Ria's still in bed?"

It's Sutton!

She offered to help me with some volleyball drills. But I didn't agree to anything. And what's she doing here? Like, right now?

Next thing I know, Mom is thumping up the stairs. I bury my head in my pillow. I hide my phone underneath it.

Fake sleep, Ria! I tell myself.

Mom bursts through the door. "Ria," she calls. "Wake up!"

"Umm . . . what?" I use my croakiest voice.

"Sutton is here to do some volleyball training with you. Did you forget?"

"No." I keep the pillow partly over my face. "But we aren't meeting until —"

"Get dressed and come downstairs," Mom says. Then she bursts back out of my room.

I mutter under my breath while I pull on leggings and a T-shirt.

"Ria!" Sutton shrieks out my name when I appear in the kitchen.

"Too much energy, Sutton," I say. "It's crazy early."

Mom glares at me and gives her head a little warning shake. She seriously needs to lighten up.

"What brings you here, Sutton?" I ask.

Sutton gives a wide smile. Then she holds out two volleyballs.

"Have some breakfast, Ria," Mom begins, "before you go train at the park." She says that in a deliberate way. I know what's up here. She's telling me I'm going to train with Sutton. Whatever happened to free choice around here?

I pop a bagel into the toaster. Then I slather cream cheese on it.

I've hardly finished eating when Mom grabs my

plate. "Away you go, Ria. We don't want to hold up Sutton any longer."

"Ria didn't hold me up much," Sutton says. "I like being early, so it's kind of my fault."

Yep, it's definitely your fault! I think.

"We're super lucky." Sutton's chirpy little voice is making my bagel and cream cheese churn in my stomach. "It's warm out today. We don't even need jackets."

"Wonderful," Mom says. "And thanks for helping Ria."

When Sutton turns the other way, Mom looks at me. Then she jerks her head — motioning me toward the door.

I grit my teeth and head outside. I follow Sutton across the street to my old elementary school. Some little kids are swinging on the monkey bars. Others are running around, kicking a soccer ball.

Sutton walks into the park. She stops at the baseball diamond.

"We're going to start here," Sutton says, "with your serves because —"

"You already told me," I say. "That even a preschooler can return my serve."

"I didn't say it quite like that," Sutton laughs. "But sure. You need to dial up that underhand serve. Or go overhand. Your call."

She points at the backstop. "This is what we'll practise serving into."

Sutton presses her back against it. Then she starts walking away from it, counting her steps.

"We need to start our serves from here." She uses her shoe to scuff out a line in the gravel. "If the ball hits above the crossbar on the backstop, then it will make it over the net in a game."

I start my usual underhand serve.

"Can I be honest with you?" Sutton asks.

Somehow, I don't think I have any choice.

"You'd be better off learning a good overhand serve. It's just three simple stages," she says. "Toss, step, hit."

"Are you sure it's that simple?" I ask.

"Not really." Sutton shrugs. "You have to practise it a ton. But that's okay."

Really? What if that's not okay by me?

"I've noticed you're left-handed," Sutton continues. "So first, put the ball in your right hand. Lift your left hand up so it's almost touching your ear. Then toss the ball toward your hitting arm."

"Okay," I say. "Then I just hit it, right?"

"Sort of," she says. "But first, you need to practise your toss. Because if you toss it too high, you're in trouble. Same if you toss it behind you."

I need to hurry her along. So I toss the ball. Then I try to hit it. But the ball drops at my feet.

"What the —?" I say.

"You have to learn the toss first," Sutton says.

"This will take forever!"

"Of course," Sutton says. "What did you think?"

I'm ready to smack her. I just want to know how to serve the stupid ball!

"Reach your hitting arm straight up," Sutton says. "That's how high you need to toss the ball. And you need to do five good tosses in a row first."

It takes me about a million tries.

"So next, I step into the ball and swing at it, right?" I ask.

"Yeah, but we're moving too fast." A frown creases Sutton's forehead.

But I'm sick of just tossing the stupid ball. So this time, I add the arm swing. But I barely connect with the ball at all. It wobbles off sideways onto the ground. Not even close to the mesh backstop!

"Make sure you're hitting the ball with the palm of your hand. Right here." Sutton points to the underneath side of her knuckles.

"Show me the whole thing again," I say.

I watch as Sutton does a smooth serve. Toss, step, hit. I watch how she follows through with her arm swing, too.

This time, I connect with the ball. It lands in the bottom of the backstop, below the crossbar.

A huge smile covers Sutton's face. She's bouncing up and down like a golden retriever puppy. "That's better," she says. "Try it again!"

I try to remember everything she said. But this time,

the ball trickles off to the side. Just when I thought I was getting it!

Sutton shakes her head. "It's because of your toss."

I grit my teeth. I'm ready to toss something at Sutton, too!

"Keep trying," she says. "Nobody gets it in just one day. It takes practise. Like, what did you think?"

I don't bother answering her.

After about ten lousy tries, I finally serve the ball into the middle of the backstop. I actually did it! Suddenly I'm doing the bouncy golden retriever thing, too. Sutton must be rubbing off on me.

But then the next three serves don't land anywhere near the backstop.

"It's okay," Sutton says. "We'll keep practising. And we'll move on to other things next time."

Hang on, I didn't say there would be a next time.

But as we leave the schoolyard, I start thinking about the energy in the gym during our first match. The gym felt alive and charged. I think almost everyone else could feel it, too. That whole volleyball vibe was taking my breath away.

As for today, my overhand serve is still pretty bad. I don't think I'll even have it by the time the season ends. But maybe I could become an okay volleyball player after all.

Maybe it's time to give that a try.

9 BOOT CAMP

Mr. Omar wasn't kidding about working us hard. It's like we're in boot camp with all the serving, passing and hitting he makes us do. Plus, he has us running and doing squats, lunges, planks, wall sits. You name it.

"For those who are feeling confident about their serves," Mr. Omar says, "you can start placing the ball. Think about the six positions where the players stand on the court."

At least I know what he's talking about. One day, Sutton explained how the positions on the court are numbered. So I know that position one is at the back right — where the server usually starts from. Position two, where the setter works from, is in front of the server. Three and four are in the middle and on the far side. Then positions five and six are in the back row. It feels good not having to pretend that I know what he's talking about. Because I wouldn't ask in front of all the others. Not in a million years.

"Sometimes in games," Mr. Omar says, "I'll want

you to serve the volleyball to a specific position on the court. So I'll use hand signals. I'll hold up fingers behind my clipboard where the other team can't see. But for now, pick a position and try serving it there."

We each grab a volleyball. I do my usual underhand serve. The ball rises in a slow arc. Then it sails to the other side. I'm setting up my next underhand serve when someone gives me a bump.

"Chicken!" Sutton frowns. "Do your overhand serve!"

"No way!" I think back to all the overhand serves I fumbled at the park. But thanks to Sutton, everyone's eyes are burning holes through me. A red-hot blush covers my face.

"Come on!" Sutton says.

She's never gonna shut up until I do this!

Toss, step, hit! I repeat the words in my head.

I toss the ball toward my left hand. Then I step into it with my right foot. When I think it's at the right height, I hit the ball. Then I bring my arm forward and down.

The ball looks like it's going over. Then it catches the tape at the top of the net. It falls back onto my side of the court.

"Pretty good!" Mr. Omar smiles.

"Almost!" Sutton is beaming.

Meg and Zina clap me across the back.

"That's amazing!" Meg says.

"Look at you go!" Zina says.

Iris and Alya are both just standing there, not saying anything. No smiles on their faces at all. I think they could be at least a little happy for me. Even though it didn't go over, it's an improvement. Then again, I guess it's not really a big deal for them.

None of my overhand serves are going over the net at all. I go back to underhand. I don't care what Sutton thinks.

Next, we volley back and forth to each other. Mr. Omar also hits balls down toward the floor and we take turns digging them back up.

"Hitting is next," Mr. Omar says. "I want to see everyone's best attacks!"

He sets the ball to us and we have to spike it over the net. Iris and Alya are slamming balls over. So are Sutton and Chen. But only one of my hits makes it over.

"Remember the trouble we had last game getting our hits past the Scorpions blockers?" Mr. Omar asks.

Some groans go up from the group.

"We're going to practise that," he says. "This time when I set you the ball, some of your teammates will be blockers. They'll be lined up across the other side of the net. You'll have to find the gaps around them."

Oh no! My hits hardly make it over the net even when no blockers are there!

When it's my turn, I back up and run hard toward

the net. I look for the gap. I think my best chance is through Eve's hands. I do my biggest arm swing and fire the ball there. But Eve stops it. The same thing happens on my next try.

My heart sinks. Just when I thought I might be getting better!

Mr. Omar's brutal conditioning exercises are next. Sweat is streaming down me by the time he calls us all in.

"So tomorrow is our next match," Mr. Omar says. "We're playing the Coyotes. Like our last match, it'll be the best-of-three games. We have a lot to build on for our second match. We're making great progress at the net. Our serves are much stronger, too."

I cringe when he mentions the serves. I won't have the nerve to do an overhand serve in an actual game. It would be an easy point for the other team if I even tried it.

I'm stuffing my kneepads and my court shoes into my bag when Sutton calls me. "Ria! Mom just texted. She's here to pick us up."

"I'll be there in a minute."

"Okay!" Sutton bounds out the door ahead of me. Iris, Alya and I are the only people left in the gym.

Iris turns to me. "Are you two besties now?"

The sneer on her face shows me what she thinks about that. But here's the thing: Sutton has been a good friend to me — even with her shrill voice and her early-morning excitement. But Iris is staring me down. I'm not brave enough to tell her that.

My skin turns itchy and I'm stumbling for words. "We're just driving together," I say. "Our moms know each other. They set it up." I try to copy Iris's cool expression.

"I get it," she says. "For a minute, I thought maybe you two were friends or something."

I shrug my shoulder as though I'm blowing off that idea.

Alya jumps into the conversation. "We're hitting up the mall later this week," she says. "Want to join us?"

I think about how Sutton offered to train me some more this week. Plus, the team has some games and more practices. I don't think we have a free day. Maybe I'm wrong about that. I probably need to check the schedule again.

"I think I can go," I say. "I have some other stuff on this week, too."

"We'll let you know when we're going," Iris says. "It'll be fun!"

As we walk outside, I think back to the few times I went to the mall with Iris and Alya. I wouldn't exactly describe it as 'fun.' But the thought of checking out the new Sephora collections and trying on some outfits at Aritzia has my heart racing.

I glance sideways at Iris and Alya. Their hair looks

a bit messy, but in a cute way. And their makeup is still flawless.

Maybe a trip to the mall with some friends is exactly what I need.

10 Coyote ATTACK

Today's game is at Cameron Woods Junior High. Some parents are driving us there. At least if I mess up, it won't be in front of many people I know. Still, my knees are shaking as I follow Saige from her mom's car.

We step into the gym and I pull on my kneepads and court shoes. The Coyotes are doing passing drills at the side. That gives us room to practise serving.

I do some underhand serves. They all go over. But they'll still be way too easy for the other team to return. I glance around me. This is my chance to try an overhand serve.

Think about the toss, I tell myself. *Not too high!*

Toss, step, hit — yes! The ball goes over the net. But it sails sideways out of bounds.

I shake my head. I'll stick with my weak underhand serve!

Mr. Omar waves us over. "The starting line-up for game one is Sutton, Alya, Olivia, Faye, Saige and

Monzi. Our setters are Sutton and Faye."

Sutton pumps her fist. Faye is shuffling from side to side. I feel bad for her. But I have my own things to worry about. Like how I suck at the net. And how the Coyotes will get easy points off my serves today, whether they are underhand or overhand.

Sutton races back after the coin toss. "We're serving first," she says. "Team cheer, everyone!"

"Ravens!" we yell, throwing our fists into the air.

I sit on the bench and take in the game. I watch how the players rotate. Their serves from position one. All the passes and sets. The attacks from the net. The player substitutions with Eve and Chen.

I realize the pieces are all coming together. Volleyball is making more sense to me.

I'm cheering hard. All the other girls are, too — except for Iris. She's just sitting with her arms crossed. I don't get that. We're up 22–14. We've had lots to cheer about. But Iris doesn't even clap or cheer when we win the first game 25–15.

Mr. Omar is beaming as everyone joins us at the bench. "That was a full team effort," he says. "Let's see that next game, too. We can't let the Coyotes force a third game. The line-up for game two is Zina, Sutton, Ria, Iris, Faye and Meg."

Please don't let me screw up! The words run through my head as I step onto the court.

The ref blows the whistle and the Coyotes server

steps up. But she sends the ball all the way through the back of the court.

"It's out!" everyone yells.

The ref signals it's our point.

We rotate and Sutton grabs the ball to serve. She glances over at Mr. Omar. Then she places the ball where he signalled: deep in the middle of the Coyotes court.

Wow! I wonder if I'll ever be able to do that.

"Get ready!" Mr. Omar calls. "It's coming back over."

"Mine!" Meg passes the ball up.

But Faye can't get to it in time. "Help!" she calls.

The ball is between Iris and me. I'm about to step back and let Iris take it. She's a better player than I am. But Iris isn't saying anything. Is she going for the ball or not?

"Whose ball?" Mr. Omar calls.

"Mine!" I rush in.

Reindeer antlers, I think. I bring both hands overhead. I set the ball. I actually set the ball to Faye — even though I had to push past Iris to do it. Faye slams the ball over the net.

As it hits the floor on the other side, we all cheer.

"Good kill, Faye!" Sutton says. "Great set, Ria!"

"That ball was mine!" Iris scowls at me. "You could have at least set it to me."

I don't know what to say. Iris hadn't called it. I couldn't

just leave the ball. I couldn't take that chance.

Sutton fires a string of serves. After that, we trade points with the Coyotes. The Ravens even get a point off my weak underhand serve. That's pretty cool!

Then Iris serves some bullets. Those points give us a huge lead!

When Zina is up to serve again, we're winning 19–11. A Coyotes player gets a good pass. Their setter pushes it across the front row.

"Mine!" Their hitter takes a big swing and sends it over the net.

"Got it!" Meg passes the ball up.

"Help!" Sutton calls.

"Mine!" The ball is low, so I do a forearm pass instead of a volley.

"Over!" everyone yells. "Three ball!"

Iris hits the ball over.

When it comes back to us, Faye passes the ball up. Sutton sets the ball to me. I don't trust my hitting arm, so I volley it over the Coyotes blockers. It hits the floor behind them. Point for the Ravens!

Hey — I'm actually helping my team!

Minutes later, Faye sets the ball to me. But the Coyotes blockers are onto me. They've formed a solid wall. I hit the ball straight into their hands. The ball bounces back to us, then slides down our side of the net. Point for the Coyotes! They're inching their way back into this!

We get the next few points back. Soon, it's 24–14.

And it's my turn to serve. Oh no! This wasn't supposed to happen!

"Game point!" the ref calls.

Sweat is streaming down the back of my shirt. I wish it was anyone but me serving. I do my lame underhand serve.

The ball has hardly left my hands when I realize I didn't hit it hard enough. I'm gritting my teeth. Will it even make it over the net?

It's a low ball. It quivers when it catches the net. Then it drops on the other side and slips down onto the court. Our point!

"Yes! Way to go, Ria!"

It's 25–14 for us! Yes!

The ref crosses her arms. "Game over! Ravens!"

My whole team has turned into Suttons — jumping and cheering. When we finally settle down, we form a line at the net. But Iris has gone back to sit on the bench instead of joining the rest of the team.

"Iris!" Mr. Omar's voice has an edge to it. "It's time to shake hands. That includes you."

Iris sighs, then joins the line.

"An amazing improvement," Mr. Omar says. "If we keep this up, we might even make it into the finals."

The finals? Really?

"For now," Mr. Omar says, "let's enjoy our win. And if everyone has a ride, I'm going to head home, too."

I'm about to leave with Saige when Sutton speaks up.

"Mom is coming to get me, Ria. She just texted. She'll drive you home, too."

I follow Sutton out into the entranceway. Iris and Alya are the only ones still waiting.

"Do you need a ride?" Sutton asks them.

"No," Alya sneers at her. "My brother's coming to get us."

"Okay," Sutton says. "I was just asking."

The tension is building. I don't know where to look or what to do.

Then Alya speaks up. "Honestly," she tosses her hair back, "I don't know why Mr. Omar took some of the girls on the team. If he went with a shorter bench, he could play the better people more often."

"Exactly!" Iris says. "He lets anyone on the team."

I swallow hard. If Mr. Omar had gone with fewer players, I wouldn't have made the team. I wouldn't have had the chance to play at all. My throat goes dry.

"He doesn't know what he's doing," Alya says.

"We're probably the first team he's ever coached," Iris says. "And it shows."

I pretend to focus hard on my phone. But Sutton turns to face them.

"You two are wrong," she says. "Mr. Omar is a good coach. And he's doing this as a volunteer. He doesn't make any extra money for coaching us."

Really? I never thought about that.

"How do you know?" Iris asks.

"My mom is a teacher," Sutton says. "So I know that's how it works."

"Sutton thinks she knows everything," Alya says.

But my mind is stuck on what Sutton said. Whenever Mr. Omar was pushing us until my muscles ached, I've kind of hated on him, too. I never said anything out loud. Still, I don't think I've been fair to him.

I wish I was brave enough to speak up, like Sutton did. But I just try to look busy while Iris and Alya complain about Mr. Omar. That he doesn't know what he's doing. That he'd be in trouble if they quit the team. And on and on.

Sutton's mom pulls up. As I'm walking to Jessica's van with Sutton, I remember something. I could have asked Iris and Alya if our trip to the mall is still on. That might have broken the tension.

I could go back and ask them. But instead, I get inside Jessica's van as fast as I can.

11 Getting VERTICAL

After we beat the Coyotes, I told Sutton I'd meet her again to practise. Sutton sure doesn't waste any time. She texts me as I'm finishing dinner.

Meet at the park in 10

I had planned to sprawl on the couch and read the new celebrity styles on *Too Cute*. But Sutton makes it hard to say no.

I text back.

Kk

I change into workout clothes and head out the door.

Sutton, of course, is already there. When she sees me, she starts pulling stuff out of her massive backpack. Some multi-coloured sticky notes, a skipping rope, a stopwatch, a measuring tape and a pen. The last thing is an old notebook. It looks like it's from grade three or something.

The words Social Studies are crossed out. In big, block letters, the words *Ria's Training* are written over top.

"First, we'll need these." Sutton holds up the sticky notes. "What colour do you want?"

"Does it matter?" I ask.

Sutton shrugs her shoulders. "Only if it matters to you," she says.

Whatever that means.

"Just give me the blue one on top." I point to it.

Sutton peels it off and hands it to me. "Take this," she says. "Then you have to jump up as hard as you can. When you're at the highest point, slap the note onto the side of the building. You have to slap it hard enough so it sticks. Otherwise, it doesn't count."

Sutton's face is super intense. It's like her whole life depends on me slapping the sticky note onto our old elementary school.

"Take a good run at it," she says.

With the sticky note clutched in my hand, I back up. I break into a run, then I throw myself upward. But I don't do a very good slap. The sticky note is hanging onto the brick by just one edge.

"Does that count?" I ask.

"Only if it sticks for . . ." Sutton screws up her face ". . . for ten seconds." She starts counting. She barely gets to six when it flutters to the pavement.

"Doesn't count," she says.

I back up and try again. This time, I do a better arm

swing. I slap the note harder and it sticks. Still, Sutton counts to ten to make sure.

"Do it two more times." Sutton pulls off two more sticky notes.

I slap both notes extra hard so she doesn't make me do it over again.

Sutton looks at them from different angles. "The pink note was the highest," she says. Then she counts the bricks below it.

"Today, your highest note was twenty-one bricks high. That's your baseline."

"My baseline?" I ask.

"Yes," she says. "The number you have to beat next time."

"What if I can't?" I ask.

"You will." Sutton writes the date and twenty-one bricks in the notebook.

Jeez, what did I get myself into?

"Next," Sutton says, "you're going to build more lower-body strength. This will help you explode upward for a better vertical jump. And that bench," she points, "is the perfect height. So watch me first."

Sutton stands on the bench. She jumps off onto the ground. When she lands, she jumps straight up, as high as she can. "Here, do a few tries."

She grabs the tape measure. "I don't quite know how to measure this," Sutton says. "Like, it's hard to know where —"

"How about if I just do five of them?" I say.

"Five isn't enough," she says. "You need to do ten."

These are harder than they look. I stop after eight. "I'm done," I say.

"No, you're not," Sutton says. "I've been counting in my head. If I were a real trainer, which I will be when I'm older, I'd make you do another ten. Because you tried to cheat."

"Okay, okay," I say. "I'll finish the ten."

Sutton writes it into her notebook.

"Next," she says, "the skipping rope." She hands it to me. Then she pulls out the stopwatch.

"Couldn't you just use your phone to time me?" I ask.

Sutton shakes her head. "This is what trainers use."

I'm about to argue. But if I do, this will take even longer.

"Start by just plain skipping. Start — now!"

Sutton keeps her eyes on the stopwatch. After I've been skipping for a while, she speaks up. "When I tell you to, skip as fast as you can. And — go!"

I speed up, keeping the rope as fast and low as possible.

"And — slow down!"

I stop and hold the skipping rope handles. "Don't stop!" Sutton says. "You still have two more speed intervals. To build your calf muscles."

I've got to hand it to Sutton. Even though she isn't

a real trainer, this feels pretty real.

"Time to cool down," Sutton says. "So, you can skip and jog — while you circle around the playground."

When I come to a stop back in front of her, a big smile covers Sutton's face.

"Did you make that last part up?" I hand her the skipping rope. "Like, about making me skip around the park?"

"Maybe," she smiles. "You can hold onto the skipping rope and some sticky notes. That way, you can practise on your own. But you'll have to keep track of everything so I can write it in here." She holds up the notebook. "You need to see the progress you're making. That will provide a lot of motivation."

Motivation. That's never been my strength.

"Okay," I say. "And if this works —"

"It will work," she says.

"Then that would be amazing," I say. "My mom could never afford to hire a trainer. So, thanks."

Sutton is beaming.

"I've learned a lot from you, and from Mr. Omar. And what you said to Iris and Alya about him being a good coach — that was true."

As we leave the park, I wish all over again that I was brave enough to speak up about stuff. But I'm not like Sutton. She doesn't seem to care what people think of her.

I kind of admire that.

12 So-Called FRIENDS

When I step out of bed the next morning, the muscles in my legs and butt are screaming. I think it's from those bench jumps Sutton made me do.

My muscles relax a bit during the day. By last class, I can walk without feeling like I'm eighty years old. I'm late leaving Science class, though. Ms. Patel is still giving students back their lab reports. I check the time. I need to hurry so I can change for practice.

Iris and Alya are hanging around outside Ms. Patel's classroom when I leave.

"Ria," Alya says, "want to come to the mall with us?"

"Sure," I say. "Text me sometime when you're going over."

"We're going today," Iris says.

That doesn't make sense.

"Like, after practice?" I ask.

"We're going right now," Alya says.

"So you're not going to practice?" I ask.

Iris raises both eyebrows. "Why would we?" she says. "Mr. Omar doesn't give us any extra game time anyway."

"Yeah," Alya says. "So we're taking a night off."

I'm looking from one to the other when Sutton appears. "You guys had better hurry up," she says. "Practice starts in —"

"Oh, god!" Iris rolls her eyes. "Are you coming with us or not, Ria?"

Images of the new nail colours at Sephora are tugging at me. And I wonder what new styles Aritzia has brought in.

"It's just one practice, Ria," Alya says. "We have lots more coming up."

"What are you talking about?" Sutton says. "You're not ditching practice, are you?" Then she turns to face me. "And you too, Ria?"

Trust Sutton — who is often kind of clueless — to figure this out!

I have been itching to hit up the mall. But here's the thing. If I go there, I know I'll be thinking about volleyball practice the whole time. I'll be wondering what the rest of the team is doing.

"No," I say to Sutton. "I'm not ditching practice. I'm just late leaving Science class."

"Oh, phew!" Sutton says. "Especially after all the work we've been doing."

"Seriously?" Iris sneers. "Are you guys pals or something?"

Alya snorts. "Sutton's a disaster. She doesn't have any friends."

The look on Sutton's face nearly flattens me. Her face crumples in and tears are pooling in her eyes. Her mouth is wide open.

I remember thinking that Sutton doesn't care what people think of her. But I can see for myself that's not exactly right. Their words really hurt her.

Suddenly, all the mean things Iris and Alya have said come rushing back to me. About Sutton and about Mr. Omar and about our team. So far, I've just stood back and let them do it.

I take a deep breath. "I can't believe you just said that." I'm trying to keep my voice steady. "You two are really good volleyball players. And your makeup and your hair are really pretty. But you suck when it comes to being nice to people."

I can tell they weren't expecting that. But I'm not done yet. I still have one more thing to tell them.

"And Sutton is my friend."

Sutton's expression softens into a teary smile.

"Let's go to practice," I tell her.

Without another word, Sutton and I take off down the hall.

We're passing through the double doors to the gym when Sutton turns to me. "Thanks," she says, "for what you said back there."

"It's true," I say. "Those two don't know how to

be nice or what it means to be a friend. I can't believe they tried to make me ditch practice. And what they said about you was really mean."

"That other thing you said, too," Sutton says. "Like, about us being friends. That . . ." her voice cracks ". . . that was nice of you. I'm not very good at making friends."

As we step inside the gym, I remember all the times Sutton drove me crazy. But she's way different from Iris and Alya. I don't think Sutton could be mean if she tried. And she's helped me out a whole ton. She's actually helped out the whole team. She'll probably keep driving me crazy sometimes. But I decide I'm okay with that.

We're pulling on our knee pads at the side bench when Sutton speaks up again.

"Volleyball is the only thing I'm good at." Her voice is still shaky. But at least she doesn't look like she's going to break into a million pieces anymore.

I'm about to tell her she's good at some other stuff, too. Just then, Mr. Omar whistles everyone over.

While we make our way there, Sutton leans in. "Should we tell Mr. Omar that Iris and Alya are ditching practice?" she asks.

"I don't think so," I say. "He's pretty smart. I think he'll figure it out for himself."

As for me, I've figured out something, too. That I did the right thing by standing up for Sutton. It doesn't matter what Iris and Alya think. Not one bit.

13 THE VOTE

Mr. Omar has been talking to Iris and Alya outside the gym for a long time. No one knows for sure how he found out about them ditching practice yesterday. But word got around the school pretty fast. That's probably because of all the pictures they posted while they were trying on clothes at the mall.

We've finished our usual warm-ups — serving, bumping, volleying, hitting at the net. Still, Mr. Omar and the two girls haven't come back inside yet.

"What should we do now?" Meg asks.

"Should we just leave?" Saige glances over at the door.

I get an idea. "I know who can train us." I point to Sutton. "Did you bring any sticky notes?"

Sutton nods and takes them out. Then she pulls some pens from her massive backpack. "Everyone, write your name on a sticky note," she says. "We're going to practise our vertical. It'll help everyone play taller at the net."

Sutton turns to me. "Ria, can you explain?"

"Sure," I say. "You take a run at the wall. Then you jump up and slap the sticky note on the wall as high as you can. And slap it hard," I continue. "Because if the sticky note falls off, Sutton freaks out and makes you do it again."

"I don't freak out!" Sutton is starting to get that collapsed-face look again. Then she sees I'm kidding, and she smiles. "You can do a demo for us, Ria."

After all my practice at the park, I do a pretty good vertical on the first try.

Sutton is beaming. "Give it a few tries, everyone. See how much higher you can slap the sticky note each time. And it has to stick!"

Mr. Omar soon appears in the gym. He gives a slow smile when he sees we're all working. "What's going on in here?" he finally asks.

"It's the sticky note challenge," Sutton says. "I found it online. It helps increase your vertical. Do you want to try?"

"Actually," he runs his hand through his dark hair, "it's been a rough day. Maybe another time."

Sutton turns back to the rest of the team. "Check how high you jumped," she says. "Count how many bricks are underneath your sticky note. That's your baseline."

While everyone counts, I smile. I knew Sutton couldn't wait to use the word 'baseline' again.

"Write that number and your name on your sticky note," Sutton says. "I'm going to collect them. We can try this again later. You can practise at home, too."

Meanwhile, Mr. Omar is pacing around the edge of the gym. "You know," he finally says to the group, "we need to talk about what happened yesterday."

Everyone pulls up on the bench.

"Being on a team can be hard," he says. "It means committing every day to trying your best. And to staying positive, no matter what." He pauses. "While I was outside talking to the two girls, I was wondering how much to share with everyone. Then I came back into the gym and found the entire team working hard without any direction from me. So I feel like I owe you an explanation."

A heavy silence has fallen over the gym.

"Yesterday, two teammates decided to skip practice. Neither one had a medical appointment. No one was sick. They just didn't feel like coming and training. Or, as they said, they 'didn't see the point.'

"When I volunteered to coach the team," Mr. Omar continues, "I saw a huge point. The skills and attitudes you learn from playing on a team can help set you up for success in life. I'm talking about persistence, dedication, work ethic and fitness. I believe in all those things, but I'm not sure what to do next. I've seen strong teams fall apart when negative attitudes start taking over. I don't want that to happen with the Ravens. But I also don't want to be unfair to the teammates who told me they 'just ditched one practice.' So I'm going to put this question to the group: what do you think we should do?"

For a long moment, everyone is completely quiet.

Then Monzi speaks up. "This isn't the first time they've been negative. Like, with you and with other players on the team."

"So it's not really about just ditching one practice," Chen says.

"It's about more than that," Faye adds.

"So what do we do next?" Mr. Omar says. "More specifically, should these girls remain on the team or not?"

No one says anything for a while.

Zina is the first to answer. "It's too bad if they miss out. But I also think they deserve to be kicked off the team."

Olivia speaks up next. "I think they forgot what they like most about playing volleyball."

"That's a good point," Mr. Omar says. "Does anyone want to tell us what they like most about it?"

"I like that we get to hang out together," Eve says.

"Me too," agrees Chen. "And I feel stronger and fitter than I did before."

Some of the girls nod.

"I hadn't done much volleyball in gym class before," Saige says. "So I've learned a whole new sport since I joined the team."

"Same here," Faye says. "And it's cool when I can do something that used to be hard for me. Like a good serve or a strong hit at the net."

A silence is hanging in the air. I can't tell if Mr. Omar is waiting for everyone to say something. And I'm not sure I want to speak up. When I signed up for the volleyball team, I really just wanted to get out of changing diapers. But I agree with what my teammates are saying. I love all those things, too.

"You guys are wrong," Meg says. "The best thing about playing volleyball is that the people around you aren't trying to kill you."

"What?" everyone says.

"My other sport is taekwondo," Meg says. "Believe me — when you're sparring with someone, it can really hurt."

Some laughs and groans go up from the group.

Sutton slowly raises her hand. "Maybe we should take a vote about whether Iris and Alya can stay on the team or not," she says. "That way, it's everyone's decision."

"I think that's a good idea," Mr. Omar says. "We'll pass a slip of paper to everyone. All you do is write 'yes' if you think they should stay on the team. Or write 'no' if you think they shouldn't stay on the team. Don't write your name. Then fold your paper and pass it to your team captain."

"Can I have someone else count these with me?" Sutton asks. "So everyone knows it was fair?"

Of course Sutton would think of every last detail!

"Good idea," Mr. Omar says.

Sutton grabs my arm and pulls me over beside her. It turns out, it's pretty easy to count the votes.

"Just about everyone voted for Iris and Alya to be off the team," Sutton says. I nod my head.

"Okay," Mr. Omar says. "We'll go with the group decision."

Sutton is biting the side of her lip. "Do I have to tell Iris and Alya? Because I'm the captain?"

"No," Mr. Omar says. "I'd like to tell them. That will give me the chance to invite Iris and Alya to try out again next year when they're in grade nine. I hope they'll make a fresh start then. I'll let them know right away."

14 Emergency MEETING

Mr. Omar calls an emergency meeting at lunch the next day.

"Our team is now down by two hitters, plus Sutton is our only setter. We've been shuffling people in and out as our second setter. We need to make some final decisions about the positions each of you will play for the rest of the season."

Everyone starts talking at once. Mr. Omar holds up his hand. "Let's start with the blockers," he says. "They're usually the people with a lot of vertical at the net."

I'm glad that Saige, Zina and Eve — the taller girls on the team — will stay in that position.

"Next up — hitters," he says. "We all have to help out at the net. But who can deliver the hardest hits for our attacks?"

An awkward silence fills the room. Our best hitters are the players we voted off the team. Iris and Alya.

"I like being a hitter," Chen says.

"You have a great hitting arm, Chen," Mr. Omar says. "Same with you girls." He points toward Faye, Meg, Olivia and Monzi.

"And now, the setters. Aside from Sutton, we still need one other person."

No one speaks up. That's when I notice something. I'm the only one who doesn't have a definite position. All my worries about if I belong on this team wash over me. My heart sinks. Just when I was starting to love this sport — and being on a team. In some ways, it would be easier if I'd ditched practice yesterday with Iris and Alya.

My eyes are burning. I need to get out of here before the tears start.

I'm reaching for my backpack when someone shrieks and grabs my arm in a tight grip. "Oh my god!" Sutton shrills. "How about Ria?"

I shake my head. Sutton needs to take the hint and just shut up.

But Sutton doesn't really take hints. "Ria should be our other setter."

"What?" My voice sounds strangled.

"I've watched you," Sutton says. "You have great hands."

Great hands?

"What?" I choke out the word.

"You know how to better the ball," Sutton says. "Like, settle it down when you're volleying it — so the hitters can do their best attack. But you've been so focussed on serving and hitting that you haven't noticed. And you're getting better at predicting the play."

I'm still fighting back tears. So I can't explain that I don't really believe the nice things Sutton is saying about me. Or how it's not a good idea for me to try playing setter at all. Instead, I just mutter that I'll think about it tonight.

But that's actually not true. I'm not going to think about it tonight. I'm done thinking for one day.

Then Sutton speaks up again. "I'll help train you, Ria!" she calls out.

Oh my god! I. Just. Can't.

★ ★ ★

When I got out of Sutton's van yesterday, I tried to stop thinking about playing setter. I really did try. But somehow, I haven't been able to think about anything else. Even when I tried to read about upcoming holiday fashion, my mind wouldn't focus. Instead, I kept thinking about the setter getting to touch the volleyball more than anyone else. And about the setter calling the plays on the court. It sounds terrifying. But I can't get it out of my head.

When our practice starts after school, Zina and I are volleying the ball back and forth.

Mr. Omar stops alongside me. "Ria," he says, "I

think Sutton is right. You could really help out the team as a setter."

I don't know what to say. When the season started, I didn't even know what a setter was. But the more I think about it, the more I feel like giving it a try. It's like how I gave volleyball a try this year, even though Mom didn't give me much choice about that. But there's a difference. When it comes to setting, I have a team who has my back — even if I mess up.

My pulse is racing, but in a good way. So before I can change my mind, I give him my answer.

"Sure," I say. "I'll try it."

"That's great," Mr. Omar says. "I'm sure Sutton will be happy to help out."

"She's a good trainer," I say.

"I agree," Mr. Omar says. "Sutton is good at more things than she realizes."

I nod. Then I remember about Mr. Omar not getting paid to coach us. About how he's doing this as a volunteer because he thinks it's important.

"By the way," I say, "thanks for coaching us."

A smile moves across Mr. Omar's face. "You're welcome," he says. "It's been a tough week. But I'm happy to coach this team."

I glance over to where the others have started serving balls. "Can Sutton start helping me with my setting?"

"Sure," Mr. Omar says. "You two can work on it for the rest of the practice."

I pull Sutton aside. I tell her what just happened.

"That's awesome!" she shrieks. "I'll pull out my training notebook."

"Not the notebook of terror!" I say.

Sutton laughs as she flies over to the bench. By the time she's back, the glee on her face tells me she's already decided on the drills we're going to do first.

15 Shake It OFF!

Sutton loses the coin toss at our next game.

"Sutton, has your luck run out?" Chen teases.

"Not a chance," Sutton says. "We'll get the serve back!"

The whistle blows and I step onto the court with Chen, Zina, Sutton, Olivia and Eve behind me.

Sure enough, Sutton was right. The first server for the Wildcats sends the ball into the net. So we get the serve back right away, plus we get the first point.

Chen serves a bullet over into the back corner. None of the Wildcats players can get to it in time.

"Ace!"

Chen is beaming. She's the strongest player on our team when it comes to Mr. Omar's conditioning work. And it shows.

Before Chen's next serve, she glances over at Mr. Omar. He's holding up one finger. Sure enough, Chen sends it to position one — to the player who

81

just served into the net. It's a great play. That girl is still shaky after missing her serve.

The Wildcats setter races back to help out her teammate. She gets the pass away. But now she can't play the second ball.

"Help!" she yells. "I'm out!"

Her teammates rush in. Another Wildcat sets the ball. The tall blocker at the net tips it over.

Olivia takes a step back and passes to Sutton. Sutton sends a long set back across to her.

"Mine!" Olivia does a big arm swing. Then she hits the ball into the net. She slumps forward.

"It's okay, you guys," Sutton calls. "Shake it off!"

The serve goes back to the Wildcats. A point goes to them, too. It's 2–1 for us.

"Ready position!" Mr. Omar calls onto the court. "Let's hear lots of talking out there!"

The next serve comes all the way over. Chen gets to it in time and passes the ball to Sutton for the set.

Zina reaches way back as though she's about to slam the ball. But at the last moment, she just volleys it up and over their blockers. It lands on the floor behind them.

"Smart play, Zina!"

The ref signals another point for us. Then she blows the whistle for Zina's serve.

Now I see why Sutton was so strict about the toss. Zina's toss is too high. When she connects with the ball, it angles sideways. It nearly hits the ref. Then it flies out of bounds. Point for the Wildcats.

"On your toes," Mr. Omar says.

The Wildcats server sends the ball into our back row. We get it over the net. When their hitter tries to attack on the next play, Eve blocks the ball. It drops to the other side of the net. The serve comes back to us again.

I gulp as our team rotates. Now, I'm in the front row.

Here it goes, I think. *I'm officially the setter!*

I try to remember everything Sutton has told me. About how I have to stay in my position on the court to start. But once the server has the ball in the air, I can move wherever I want. And that's to position two — the right side of the court by the net. I need to get ready to slide over there.

The whistle blows and Sutton serves a bullet. I rush to position two — just in time to pick up Chen's pass.

"Mine!" I yell.

I set the ball to Eve, but it's not quite where she wants it. She just sends the ball over the net with an overhand pass.

"Free ball!" the other team yells.

Free ball, as in, I made it too easy for the Wildcats. Ugh!

When the Wildcats middle blocker tips the ball, it's back on our side. And I have to go for it!

I pop the ball up into the air with an underhand pass. But now, I can't take the second ball. I can't set it to the hitters.

But what do I say?

"Help!" Sutton yells from the back row. "Setter's out!"

Thank god Sutton covered for me!

Olivia rushes in and sets the ball. Eve tips it over. The ball drops to the floor on the other side.

"Yay!"

"Great play out there!"

My whole team is going nuts. The Wildcats didn't expect Eve to do that!

Sutton is shrieking her head off! We keep driving hard — trying to keep the momentum going.

The Wildcats get some points on their next serves, but we're gaining a big lead. We're up 21–13. That's good, because I'm still trying to figure out the different sets that our hitters like. Olivia likes higher sets. Chen likes low, quick sets so she can slam them in hard from outside. It's a lot to remember, especially while the game is unfolding all around me. I don't know how Sutton makes it look so easy.

I start breathing a bit easier when we're up 24–16.

The ref blows her whistle. "Game point!" she calls.

Olivia scoops up the ball to serve. She's been serving deep into their court all game. This time, she surprises them by sending the ball into their front row.

Shake It Off!

A Wildcats player picks up the pass. But I think Olivia has caught her off guard. The player just reacts and sends it back over to us with a soft underarm pass.

"Free ball!" Mr. Omar yells.

Sutton has lots of time to get under the ball. She passes it to me.

"Got it!" I say.

"Over here!" Chen calls.

I set her a low, quick ball. Chen times her approach well and slams it over the net.

"Great hit!" everyone shouts from the bench. They're all cheering hard as the Wildcats scramble to dig up Chen's ball.

From the back row, a Wildcats player rushes in. But she doesn't get a solid pass away.

"Help!" her setter calls.

One of her teammates settles down the ball. But the hitter isn't ready. The ball lands in the net, then it drops to the floor.

Yes! It's 25–16 for us. We win!

"Game!" The ref signals by crossing her arms in front of her chest.

Suddenly, all the Ravens are jumping up and down in centre court. Our feet hardly touch the ground as we bounce over to the bench.

When the second game starts, it seems the Wildcats have already given up. The momentum from the first game carries us through the second one, too. We take it 25–14.

"Two games straight!" Sutton yells.

When the group hug breaks up, we all step to the back line. The rest of our team joins us as we shake hands with the Wildcats.

"That was an excellent team effort, Ravens," Mr. Omar tells us. "Ria, your setting was great! You handled your first match beautifully!"

I can feel the smile stretching across my face. "I had some good coaching." I nudge Sutton, who pumps her fist into the air.

"That was a big win," Mr. Omar says. "We had a slow start to the season. But I've checked the standings. If we keep this up, we could even land in the championship match."

The championship match? Being on the team with the other girls has been more fun than I ever thought. But just thinking about the extra pressure that would go with playing in a big match like that makes my knees shake. Now that I'm one of the setters, I'll definitely be out on the court if that happens.

"Oh, wow!" Faye says.

"That would be so cool!" Monzi adds.

"For now," Mr. Omar says, "everyone is doing the right things. Playing hard, staying positive and helping the team."

I'm trying to listen to Mr. Omar. But my thoughts are still jumping around.

As we leave the gym, Sutton seems to pick up on the vibe I'm giving off. She nudges my shoulder.

"You're not scared, are you?" she asks.

"Who — me?" I try to ignore how my voice shakes.

"Don't worry," Sutton says. "We've got this."

I hope she's right about that.

16 Hanging OUT

We're crammed together on the couch in Eve's living room. The whole team is here except for Zina, Monzi and Faye.

I've just sat down when Zina bursts through the door — her lunch bag in her hand.

"Zina!" I say. "Over here!"

I scoot over to make room for her. But it nearly pushes Chen off the other end of the couch.

"I can't believe you just did that!" Chen laughs.

I start to giggle, and I can't stop. When Chen and Zina flop down onto the rug, I slide off the couch and join them. We all open our lunch bags.

The door to the study opens and Eve's dad steps out. He's running his hands through his hair. It's all sticking up at the front.

"Dad," Eve points to the mirror on the wall. "Check out your hairstyle."

Mr. Thomas takes a look. "I like it that way," he says with a goofy grin.

Mr. Thomas works from a home office. Since Eve's house is close to the school, we usually eat lunch at her place. I think her dad is used to seeing our whole team sprawled out in his living room.

"Were we being too loud?" Sutton asks.

"It's okay," Mr. Thomas says. "I needed a break anyway." He walks through into the kitchen. I can hear some dishes clattering and cupboard doors closing.

Minutes later, Monzi and Faye burst through the front door. They shake the snow from their coats and drop them onto the bench.

"Wait till you guys see what I made!" Monzi reaches into her tote bag and pulls out a container.

"Brownies?" Olivia says. "Please tell me you made brownies again!"

Monzi pulls off the lid. "Yup, my world-famous brownies!"

Everyone rushes in.

"You're the best, Monzi!"

"Oh my god — I love these!"

While we chow down, I show Saige, Chen and Zina my favourite blogs. "Ooh! Look at that hoodie," Saige says.

"I know," I say. "I want one in every colour. I love the leggings, too."

Sutton glances over at my phone. "Those leggings are okay," she shrugs. "No big deal. And, hey — what's everyone doing over the holidays?"

"I'm sticking around," Faye says between bites.

"Me too," I say.

"Same with me," Meg says. "I have a taekwondo tournament."

"I'll be gone for part of the holidays," Saige says. "All my cousins are in Calgary. We're going there for New Year's."

"I'll be away, too," Sutton says. "We're visiting my grandparents in Palm Springs."

I've hardly even thought about the holidays. My head has been too wrapped up in volleyball. Even though it's cold and snowy outside, Sutton has dialed up our training sessions.

That night after supper, Sutton and I head to the park. Like always, I work on my vertical. I don't know how many sticky notes I slap against my old elementary school. I've improved a lot since the first time I tried. I also run some sprints. Then we practise serving into the backstop.

Sutton is serving one bullet after another. The wire mesh is rattling against the metal posts that hold it in place. It's not going so well for me, though. My first two serves drop too soon. Then the third one hits above the crossbar.

"Yes!" I say.

"Right on, Ria!" Sutton says. "Keep going!"

But my next two serves fly sideways.

Back to underhand for me! I think.

I pretend I don't hear Sutton's heavy sigh when I switch back.

Sutton has me do some straight sprints and zigzag sprints. She says this will help me get to the second ball quickly so I can set it. She's still timing me and measuring my results. It's actually cool to see how I'm improving.

Wisps of snow are swirling through the air. It's dark by the time we say good-bye.

When I get home, Mom is studying in the kitchen. I make a smoothie, then I pull up at the table with her.

"That's really disgusting." I shudder as I point at the pictures of mouth sores in her textbook.

"It gets better," she says. "I'm studying head and neck anatomy next."

"Gross!" I shove a sweaty wisp of hair back off my face.

Mom laughs. "How did your training go?"

"Intense," I say. "Sutton is almost as tough as Mr. Omar."

"I think the training has been good for you," she says. "I'm sure it's been good for Sutton, too."

"How do you mean?" I ask between slurps of my smoothie.

Mom hesitates before she speaks. "Jessica worries about Sutton. Sutton doesn't always mix well with the other kids. She's never had many friends."

I let Mom's words sink in. "I've noticed that," I say.

"She isn't always easy to be around. But she's really nice. And she's thoughtful."

Mom nods. "I think the training she's doing with you means more to her than any of us realize. I like that you're being a friend to her. She's needed that."

"I've needed her help, too," I say as I pull out my phone. Then I notice how Mom's eyes have landed on it. "I was just going to check some YouTubes," I say. "There are some good volleyball tips online."

Mom smiles. "Do they offer 'best makeup tips for game day'?"

My jaw starts to tighten. Then I realize she's joking.

"For sure," I joke back. "I'm looking for the post about how all the trendy volleyball players style their knee pads. Nothing screams fashion like knee pads and court shoes do."

Then I go back to searching for volleyball tips. Especially for more ideas about serving. But really, I already know the answer. I need to keep practising.

I'm just glad I have a team that supports me — even though I keep handing points and easy plays over to the other team. On every single serve. Maybe someday, I'll get this serving thing figured out. Hopefully before the season ends.

17 SEMI-FINAL

The matches are piling up behind us. A win against the Panthers in two games straight.

A loss to the Dynamos after three games.

A win, in two straight games, against the Rattlers.

A heartbreaking loss in three games to the Dragons.

A nail-biter of a win against the Storm in three.

Today, we're playing the Cheetahs. They took the first game 25–20. Then we came back and won the second game, 25–21. I thought I was going to have heart failure before we finished the game.

The tie-breaker is about to start. My voice is shot from yelling. This is the semi-final match. Whoever wins is playing in the championship in four days. The next fifteen points for either team will decide it!

"Stay sharp out there," Mr. Omar says to us. "Keep the momentum going. Let's finish this off!"

As game three starts, the energy in the gym is electric. We're all completely focused. Earlier in the season, we didn't always try too hard. If the ball looked like it was tough to get to, we sometimes just gave up. But now, we do anything to keep the volleyball from hitting the floor. We all have some bruises to show for it.

Sutton is standing across from me. "Team cheer, everyone!" she says. "Three, two, one —"

"Ravens!" We throw our fists into the air.

When the ref blows the whistle, Meg, Sutton, Zina, Chen, me and Saige step onto the court.

"Service!" the ref calls, then blows the whistle.

Their team captain sets up her serve. Then she blasts it over the net.

"Mine!" Saige calls. She passes the ball up.

"Got it!" Sutton pushes the set over to Chen. Chen takes a run at the net, but her timing is off. The ball barely makes it over. A front-row Cheetahs player pops it up into the air. Then their setter does something that takes my breath away. She does an amazing back set to the hitter behind her.

Wow, she switched up her sets perfectly! I had no idea she was going to do that until the very last moment.

But right now — *Focus, Ria!* I tell myself.

Their hitter pounds the ball over the net.

"Go, Saige!" we yell.

Saige rushes to get there. Her pass is off, though. Sutton can't get to it.

"Help!" Sutton yells.

Meg pops the ball up for her.

"Mine!" Sutton does a massive arm swing. She delivers a killer hit.

When it smacks onto the floor, our bench erupts in cheers.

"What a swing, Sutton!" My voice is raspy.

The serve comes back to our end. Sutton scoops up the ball. She blasts it deep into the other end with her serve.

A Cheetahs player in the back row passes the ball up. Her setter does a low, quick set to the power hitter. But the hitter doesn't connect well on it. The ball flies out of bounds.

The serve comes back to Sutton. For the first time I can remember, Sutton's serve goes sideways. It sails into the Ravens bench.

"It's okay, Sutton," I say. "Shake it off!"

Mr. Omar has talked to our team about how important it is to stay positive. We have to treat each rally like it's a new game.

The next Cheetahs server sends the ball into the middle of our court. Saige passes it forward. I do a quick set, then Chen slams the ball. The Cheetahs blockers jump for it, but the ball tips off their hands and hits the court behind them.

We're the first to get to the mid-point of the third game. We're up 8–6. My stomach is in knots while we switch sides for the final end.

For the next few rallies, I can't believe how evenly matched our two teams are. My heart is racing when it's my turn to serve. I feel Mr. Omar's eyes on me. He maybe wants me to do an overhand serve. But I can't take the chance. The score is 11–10 for us. I need this ball over the net!

I heave a huge sigh when my underhand serve makes it over. But as usual, the other team gets a good pass on it. When they hit it back over, Zina's pass angles off her forearm. It flies out of bounds and hits the far wall.

Everyone gasps. It's 11–all. The game only goes to 15. We don't have much time!

The Cheetahs server fires the ball over. Chen picks up the pass. She sends it to Sutton in the front row.

Sutton sets the ball to Meg, and she slaps it over the net. The Cheetahs player closest to it sends the ball back into our zone with an underarm pass. But Saige blocks it. The ball flies back onto their side.

It's tight against the net. Two Cheetahs players are swinging at it, but the ball skids down the net. It lands on the floor.

It's 12–11 for us!

"Too soon to celebrate," Mr. Omar calls. "We have more work to do!"

Saige steps up to serve. Mr. Omar is signalling with four fingers. Saige gets a great weight on the ball. She sends it right down the line. The player seems to panic and hits the ball directly back over the net.

Our players are all yelling, "It's out!"

Chen draws her hands back so the ref can see she isn't touching the ball. The line judge raises the flag into the air.

Yes — out of bounds. Point for us!

We're up 13–11. When the ref blows the whistle, Saige serves the ball to the same player. The girl seems to freeze at first. Then she can't get under the ball in time. It drops to the floor beside her. It's 14–11 for us. Just one more point to go!

I look over to see if the Cheetahs coach is going to call a time out. Saige is a hot server. If I were him, I'd try to interrupt the flow of the game. Sure enough, he calls for a time out.

We bounce over to the bench. Mr. Omar is starting to say something — and we all know what it is.

"Too soon to celebrate yet!" Monzi uses a deep voice, imitating Mr. Omar.

Everyone bursts out laughing.

"Still more work left to do!" Faye adds her imitation.

A smile is tugging at the corner of Mr. Omar's mouth. "I guess I don't have to say much at all," he says. "Great serving, Saige. Now, go finish this off."

She does. She scores an ace on a serve that lands in the far back corner.

A moment later, we're all hugging and jumping up and down on the court.

Sutton is jumping highest of all. "Championships — here we come!"

Mr. Omar waits a few moments. "Amazing teamwork," he says. "It sure looked like everyone was having fun."

Wow. I never thought volleyball was fun when I first started playing. But it's true. Fun and exciting! Sparks were flying around the gym during the final minutes of the game!

"Before everyone leaves," Mr. Omar says, "there's one more thing. Since our gym is small, we'll be playing the championship match at the high school."

"At Nelson Gates High School?" Chen asks.

Mr. Omar nods. "They have a fantastic gym. There's lots of room around the court for the servers and lots of space for spectators. Everyone can invite extra family and friends to cheer us on."

Then the comments start. About getting to check out our future high school. About how cool it will be to play there. About how some high-school coaches might even be watching for new players to recruit onto their teams next year.

I glance over at Sutton. She's still bouncing. But she's also giving off a calm, confident vibe. She looks more than ready for the final match. I just hope I am, too.

18 Playing It SAFE

Sutton and I train hard on the weekend. We slap tons of sticky notes against my old school. We run sprints. And we practise serving into the backstop.

Sutton serves one bullet after another. The wire mesh rattles against the metal posts. She shakes her head whenever I do an underhand serve.

"You know what your problem is, Ria?" Sutton doesn't give me a chance to answer. "You play it too safe."

"Why is that a bad thing?" I ask.

"Because it holds you back," Sutton says. "You don't try stuff like serving overhand in a game. Even though you could probably do it."

I think ahead to our championship match. "It's not going to happen. Especially not next week during the championship. There's too much at stake!"

"See what I mean?" Sutton says. "And what about that back set that rocked your world last game?"

I think back to how the Cheetahs setter surprised us by setting the ball backward. "Wait!" I say. "Sutton, you're freaking me out. I didn't even tell you —"

"You didn't have to tell me. I saw your face. You could do back sets, too. Here, I'll show you."

Sutton makes me practise until I can set the ball behind me. The whole time, she's watching my hand position. And she stops me if I'm arching my back.

"You have to be sneaky," she says. "You can't let the other team know you're going to set the ball behind you."

Then she shows me some other setting techniques that she calls top secret. "Those," Sutton says, "are in case you decide to step out of your safe zone next week."

As we're leaving the park, I ask Sutton a question. "Do you ever wonder what would have happened if Iris and Alya had stayed on the team?"

Sutton pauses for a moment. "We could use their serving and hitting arms. But we wouldn't be in the championship if they were on the team. We wouldn't have worked together so well this season."

I nod and take a gulp from my water bottle. As I walk up the driveway, I think about how I nearly went with Iris and Alya when they ditched practice. If I'd gone to the mall with them, I'd be off the team, too.

The shudder that passes through me has nothing to do with the cold, biting wind.

That was a close call! I realize.

★ ★ ★

"This place is massive!" Zina says as we step inside the high school.

"I'll never find my way around here next year." Chen swerves around a group of students.

"Don't let it throw you," Mr. Omar says. "This is super exciting."

"And terrifying," Monzi says.

The butterflies in my stomach are telling me the same thing.

When we walk through the double doors to the gym, my eyes sweep to the upper bleachers. The parents from Yana Malko Junior High are sitting together. Mom will come after her last class. She kept asking me which games I'd be playing in. I told her I'm on the court all the time because I'm a setter. I don't think she really gets it.

Up above, another group is filing in. They're wearing Scorpions hoodies and sweatshirts. Moments later, cheers echo down onto the court when their team walks into the gym. I remember how the Scorpions crushed us at the start of the season. I'd mostly put them out of my mind. Until today.

"Go start our regular warm-ups," Mr. Omar says.

We grab some volleyballs and start serving. We do our passing and hitting warm-ups, too. The ref calls the captains over to shake hands. Then the coin arcs upward and lands at their feet.

Sutton returns to our bench. "They took first serve."

"That's okay," Mr. Omar says. "We'll get our defence to work right away. The line-up for game one is Sutton, Eve, Faye, Ria, Saige and Monzi."

The ref blows the whistle. My heart is pumping as their server fires the ball. Monzi hustles over and passes it to me.

"Mine!" I yell as I set it to Faye.

"Got it!" Faye swings hard. The ball sails over the Scorpions blockers, but their second row is ready.

"On your toes!" Mr. Omar calls. "It's coming back!"

They send the ball deep across the court. Saige runs for it and passes to me.

"Faye!" I set the ball to her again.

Faye spikes it between their blockers. Their back-row player gets away a solid pass.

"Mine!" their setter calls.

Their outside hitter winds up. It's coming back hard!

"Block it!" I yell.

Eve and Faye jump together. The ball smacks off Eve's hand and drops onto the other side.

Yes! It's 1–0 for us. But they sure made us work for it!

The whole first game goes that way. None of the points come easily. The rallies go on forever. The pressure builds with each touch on the ball.

It's 12–10 for us when it's my turn to serve. Sutton's words replay in my mind. "Your problem is you play it too safe."

But this game is important! I can't take a chance.

The gym has grown quiet. I can feel everyone's eyes on me. I step behind the line. I pop the ball up and do my underhand swing.

The ball goes over. But the Scorpions player gets an easy pass away and then they attack hard.

When the ball comes back over, I can barely dig it up. My pass to Sutton is shaky, but she gets away a set to Monzi. The Scorpions blockers are towering in front of Monzi. Their hands look like snow shovels. One of them pushes the ball back onto our court. It hits the floor.

Point for them.

We're exchanging points — one for us, then one for them. But then, the Scorpions take three straight points. It's 17–14, and they're running away with this game!

At the next whistle, Mr. Omar calls a time out. "We're holding back at the net. I need you to be fearless out there with the attacks. The Scorpions have nothing on us."

I don't hear the rest of what he says. The blood is pulsing in my temples as I follow the team back onto the court.

The ref blows the whistle. The Scorpions server drills the ball over the net.

Faye runs for it. "Mine!" she yells, but she doesn't get good contact on the ball. It's sailing out of bounds!

"I've got it!" I yell.

"Follow her in!" Mr. Omar yells from the sidelines.

I can hear Saige running behind me. I dive across the floor, sliding on my stomach. My face nearly smashes into the side wall, but I get there in time. I form a pancake on the floor with my hand. The ball lands on my hand and bounces up.

Saige sends the ball back over with a big underarm pass.

Yes! I helped keep it in play!

"Free ball!" the Scorpions yell.

The Scorpions setter picks up the pass. But she pushes the ball too far. It flies out of bounds.

"Great rally!" Mr. Omar calls from the bench. "Now, let's use this!"

At that point, the energy does a crazy swing. Because before long, we're up on the Scorpions, 19–18.

Saige serves some bullets. We get the next two points.

It's 21–18 for us. We need to finish this off!

Saige steps up to serve again. The Scorpions are backing up. They're expecting her to serve another hard ball deep into the court. But this time, she sends a lighter one over. Their setter has to play it.

"I'm out!" she yells. "Help!"

A blocker steps in and tips the ball over on the second touch. It hits the floor. I clench my teeth. None of us saw that coming.

"Shake it off!" Sutton says. "We're good!"

We come back and take the next point. And now it's Monzi's serve.

Monzi fires the ball deep into their centre court. When a Scorpions player sends the ball out of bounds, the serve comes back to us.

Monzi scores an ace on the next serve. Nobody gets a touch on it at all. The score is 24–19 for us. This is game point! The Scorpions coach calls a time out.

"Come on, Monzi," everyone calls as the time out ends. "You've got this!"

The whistle blows and Monzi serves another bullet. Still, the Scorpions don't go down without a fight. They score two more points. We still need one more point to win.

Sutton steps up to serve. She sends the ball straight down the line. The Scorpions player sends the ball out of bounds. That means —

"Ravens!"

"We won!"

The six of us hug on the court. We bound back to the bench for more hugs, all our faces lit up.

"That was great teamwork," Mr. Omar says. "We need to keep that energy going for the next game. We can't underestimate the Scorpions one bit."

I glance over at them. The Scorpions look more determined than ever.

19 The Pressure BUILDS

We switch sides for game two. Mr. Omar reads out the new line-up: Sutton, Zina, Meg, me, Olivia and Chen.

Just like last game, we mostly trade points. One point for the Scorpions, then one for us. It's 15–14 for them. Olivia, Meg and I are stacked in the centre of the court. We're ready to run to our positions once the Scorpions serve is in the air. Meg is standing on one foot. She's rotating her other foot in circles.

"Did you hurt your —"

That's all I get to say before the ball comes over the net. I rush to position two. Chen passes the ball to me there. I set it over to Olivia, but the Scorpions blockers are onto her. They're like a brick wall on the other side.

For the next rallies, we can't get anything past them. They're gaining points on us with their block. We're too afraid to even try hitting. We keep sending one free ball after another back at them. Meanwhile, they're attacking hard.

The Pressure Builds

I can't keep setting to Olivia. The Scorpions blockers are guarding her too closely. I have to mix up the sets. On the next play, I know what I have to do. I take a deep breath. Then I back set the ball to Meg.

My set is a little off, and Meg has to run for it. She takes a step toward the net. Then her ankle hits the post. She crumples to the floor. The ball drops beside her.

"Oh no! Meg!"

Everyone rushes to her.

Mr. Omar calls for a substitution. Faye is standing beside him. "Number three in for number twelve," he says.

Faye gives Meg a quick hug as she steps onto the court. Meg limps off to the bench.

Suddenly, it feels like all the air got sucked out of the gym. Meg is injured. We're down 21–14.

By the time the ref calls 'game point,' the Scorpions have pretty much finished us off. Minutes later, they score the final point they need. They win game two 25–16. The Scorpions have just forced the tie-breaker game for the championship.

After our great start, how could we have let this happen?

★ ★ ★

Between games, Meg explains about hurting her ankle in taekwondo.

"It wasn't that bad," she says, "until I cracked it into the post."

Now that Meg's court time has ended, our bench just got shorter. Maybe if Iris and Alya were still on the team . . .

Nope! I won't go there.

"We let the pressure get to us last game," Mr. Omar says. "Then we gave up when it got hard, when the Scorpions were blocking our hits. We seemed to decide it was over then. So that's exactly what happened. But now, we have a third game. This is our chance to get it back."

I can tell from Mr. Omar's voice that he believes we can take this last game. But the others don't look convinced. I'm not sure I am, either.

But then I remember something. We don't have much time. I need to speak up.

"Remember what we said we loved most about playing volleyball?" I look at my teammates. "We need to play like those things matter."

Sutton nods. "Ria is right. Last game, we didn't prove we deserve to be here. So now, we're going to remind the Scorpions they're up against a strong team. And that the Ravens don't back down — no matter what."

"Exactly," Mr. Omar says. "We're going to compete hard for every point out there. And to push through when it gets tough. We have a job ahead of us, and we're going to get it done."

For a long moment, nobody says anything. Even in this loud gym, a sort of stillness has settled around us.

Then Sutton speaks up. "Fists into the middle!" she says. "Three, two, one —"

"Ravens!"

When the tie-breaker game starts, we come out with a lot of jump. The Scorpions push back hard. But we take the first three rallies.

Monzi steps up to serve, and Mr. Omar holds up four fingers. Monzi sends it there — straight down the line to position four. Their player hangs back, watching to see if it's going out of bounds. By the time she moves to play it, she doesn't get a good pass away.

"Help!" the setter calls.

Two players rush in. The first pops the ball up. The other one passes it over the net.

"Free ball!" Mr. Omar yells. "Use it!"

Sutton passes the ball to me. I push it long to give Chen space to run at it.

Chen swings at the ball. But their blockers are back in action at the net. They knock the ball over to our side. Chen digs it straight up.

"Got it!" I do a short, quick set. Zina slams the ball over before the Scorpions can respond.

"Yeah!" We're all yelling our heads off.

It's 4–0 for us!

"You've got this," Sutton calls, as Monzi starts her next serve.

Monzi's ball has a lot of float on it. The Scorpions hesitate, trying to see where it's going. Then they regroup on the pass. Their setter flies in and does a short set. Her blocker reaches up and knocks the ball over behind our front row.

Eve barely keeps the ball in the air. It's too far for me to get to!

"Help!" I yell.

Sutton pops the ball straight up. Chen goes for the big hit — but the ball tips the net and lands out of bounds.

The Scorpions cheer hard as they take back the serve.

It's okay, I tell myself. *We're still up on them.*

But we aren't up for long. The Scorpions are clawing their way back into this game. They get to 8 points before we do. We switch sides for the final half of the tie-breaker. My legs are shaky and weak. It's 8–7 for them. We need to pull this back together!

The Scorpions are on fire with their serves. When two balls drop by Zina, Mr. Omar subs Saige in. She's fresh and she makes some tough passes.

When the rally comes to Chen, she switches up her hit. She finds a gap between the blockers and slams the ball over.

Yes! It's tied at 10 points apiece.

But it's far from over. The massive Scorpions blocker is towering over all of us. Who knows if we can get another ball past her!

The Pressure Builds

It feels like I can hardly breathe. The Ravens and the Scorpions keep exchanging points. None of our games all season have been so evenly matched.

It's tied up again at 13–13, and they have the serve.

I wish I was in the back row. It would be better and safer for the team if Sutton was setting instead of me. She's far steadier and she knows more plays than I do.

I glance at the Scorpions hitter across the net from me. I've noticed that her vertical isn't great. Then I remember one of the new plays Sutton and I practised on the weekend. It might work — if I can pull it off.

I'm not sure I can do it. But we need to turn this game around. This might be the only chance I get.

20 The Icing ON THE CAKE

Monzi passes the ball to me. I know I have to go for it. And I have to do it right now!

I can hear Sutton's words in my head. *Slap the sticky note!*

I jump as high as I can. I keep both hands up until the last moment. Then, when the ball is by my left ear, I turn my hand. I don't set the ball at all. Instead, I slam it down toward their court with my left hand.

A moment later, the most beautiful sound in the world reaches my ears. The sound of the ball smacking the floor on the other side of the court. Yes!

"Great dump, Ria!" Sutton yells.

"Nailed it, Ria!"

"They didn't see that coming!"

It's true. They didn't expect me to send the ball over on the second touch. The turn-and-burn worked. It was a high-risk move, and it paid off! A roar of cheering reaches us down on the court. We're up 14–13!

The Icing on the Cake

The Ravens do a quick hug in the centre of the court.

"Your trainer is super proud of you!" Sutton says.

I'm shaking too hard to answer her. Because what if that hadn't worked? And it's not just that — I'm serving next.

Oh my god!

"Game point!" the ref says.

A wave of heat washes through me. My throat goes dry as it hits me — my team could win the championship on this point. And it starts with my serve.

My serve!

I'm waiting to scoop up the ball when the Scorpions coach does exactly what we expect. Calls a time out.

We hustle over to our bench.

"They're just trying to get under your skin, Ria!" Zina says.

I swallow hard. Because their time out is working. The pressure is eating away at me. I'm ready to bolt from the gym!

"Everyone is going to stay strong," Mr. Omar says. Then he looks at me. "This is just one of many serves you've done, Ria. You can do this!"

But can I really? All season long, my serves have been easy for the other team to receive. I know the Scorpions will take advantage if we give them the smallest chance. And that starts with my serve — for game point.

The ref blows the whistle to end the time out. I startle as though the whistle blast just punctured a hole through my eardrums.

Sutton slips over beside me. "You know what to do, Ria," she says. "Show those Scorpions what you've got!"

Then she throws her fist down. "Everyone in! Three, two, one —"

"Ravens!"

We line up and the ref signals us back onto the court. I scoop up the ball and step behind the line.

After the whistle, I'm about to start my underhand serve. Then Sutton's words from the weekend are running through my head.

Your problem is you play it too safe.

I take a deep breath. In my mind, I replay everything Sutton taught me about overhand serving. Then I go for it.

Toss, step, hit!

The ball goes over! It actually goes over, and it has a bit of heat to it. It lands centre court. The Scorpions have to scramble to get to it in time.

Yes! I made it tougher for them!

When they send it back across the net, it's a free ball.

Zina picks up the pass. She sends it to Sutton in the front row.

But Sutton doesn't set it, like the Scorpions probably expect. She does her own turn-and-burn on the ball.

She slams it across the net so fast and so hard that none of the Scorpions can even touch it.

Suddenly, the Ravens are all bouncing and hugging and shrieking. I want to join in. But I can't celebrate too soon. I need to see it first for myself.

The ref crosses her arms in front of her body. That's the signal I'm waiting for. Game over!

"The champions!"

"We won!"

"We did it!"

Our cries echo through the gym. I'm swept up into the massive group hug in the centre of the court. I jump up and down with my teammates and wipe away tears, too. Even Meg is doing careful hugs with the team.

"Great overhand serve, Ria!" Sutton says. "You went for it!"

"It was terrifying," I choke out.

Sutton smiles. "Still, you did it!"

"Yeah." My knees give a wobble. "And how about you? That turn-and-burn . . ."

Sutton shakes her head. "It was a last-minute decision. I didn't think the Scorpions would expect a turn-and-burn from our other setter. I was just following your lead."

Really? Following my lead? So I had something to do with Sutton's game-winning move?

I can't find any words. I have nothing to say at all

as our team bounces over to the bench.

"That was incredible, girls!" Mr. Omar says. "Just incredible!" He says other things, too, but it's too noisy in the gym to hear him.

Then, a perfect day gets even better because they bring out the medals.

The two teams line up to face each other. It feels like a movie is playing out around me. But the best thing about it is I'm part of this movie, too.

My whole team claps hard for the Scorpions when the officials give them their silver medals. Then out come the gold medals. Every nerve in my body is quivering. It feels like the roof is going to blow right off. The sweaty gym takes on a bright new glow.

Remember this moment, Ria! I tell myself.

"Thanks," I tell the official when she slips the gold medal over my head. Then I hunch my shoulders. I need to feel the satiny cord against the back of my neck. The weight of the pendant against my Ravens jersey sends an extra buzz through me.

Our parents are piling onto the court. We hand them our phones so they can take team pictures. We do some serious poses. Then we do some goofy poses, like with our medals clenched between our teeth.

"I don't want to go," Sutton says as our team stands up. "I don't want this season to end."

I know exactly what she means.

"It won't end quite yet," Mr. Omar says. "I've

arranged for pizza and cake for our athletes."

Athletes. Wow, I never thought of myself as an athlete. But with a full season of volleyball behind me and a medal around my neck, I realize that's exactly what I am.

"And now," Mr. Omar says, "it's definitely time to celebrate!"

Most of us have lost our voices. Still, we find a way to yell and cheer even more.

I look over at Mom. A big smile covers her face. She's the one who pushed me onto a school team, so she deserves some cake, too. I'll even try to save her a piece with extra icing.

Then it hits me that the volleyball season is really over. I'll have some free time again. Time when I can find out what jeans and tops are in style. And which lip colours and nail polishes are on trend.

But I can read about those things later. I'll also serve some volleyballs. I'll practise my setting, too. And I'll keep slapping sticky notes onto the wall with Sutton and the rest of my friends.

Because I have to make sure I'm ready for next season.

ACKNOWLEDGEMENTS

A dedicated team of hitters, blockers and setters converged around me while I was writing *Volleyball Vibe*. A warm thank you to the entire team at James Lorimer & Co., including Carrie Gleason for her confidence in me. Extra special thanks to Kat Mototsune, cherished friend and editor, who helps me write my best possible stories.

I am also grateful to Julie Noel of Volleyball Alberta for directing my volley (sorry!) of questions throughout the organization. Jim Plakas, director, was an invaluable source of information. His detailed responses to my questions enhanced this story. Many thanks, Jim, for your generosity and expertise.

Joel Brown also supported my dream of writing this book for those who love volleyball, and for those who will hopefully discover it. An experienced referee, Joel painstakingly explained the different volleyball systems played at local junior high schools. I am inspired and humbled by Joel's knowledge, and by his sensitivity toward the athletes of various ages on the court before him. Thanks to Alison Hughes, my dear friend and colleague, for connecting me to Joel.

In many elementary and junior high schools, young athletes are introduced to volleyball by a "triple ball" system to help develop young players and to increase participation. I did not feature triple ball in *Volleyball*

Acknowledgements

Vibe, however, as I followed the guidelines for junior-high teams within the Edmonton Public School Board. Had Ria played volleyball the previous year on a junior team, her games would have adhered to the triple ball format.

For Ria's final match, I deviated somewhat from protocol. Edmonton's junior-high teams play the best of five games for the championship. For story purposes, however, Ria and the Malko Ravens played the best of three games (also called sets), just as they did in the regular season. I hope I captured some additional excitement by moving the match to a larger gym at Ria's neighbouring high school. Go, Ravens!

On the "home court," my solid, loving team includes my nephew, Matt Spafford, who remains the best teen-voice reader I could possibly ask for. Via rapid-fire texts, Matt helps ensure my teen characters sound suitably current. Any errors or miscues are mine alone.

Thanks also to my daughter, Shannon Fitz, whose information about her dental hygiene program helped me write the character of Ria's mom. Like Ria, I avoided looking at the more graphic diagrams in Shannon's textbooks, or thinking too closely about the early attempts to freeze classmates' mouths. Still, I couldn't be a prouder or more grateful mom.

Over the years, my daughters' volleyball exploits have taken my family throughout Canada, and their enthusiasm inspired *Volleyball Vibe*. Anna and Shannon were also my earliest readers, and their input made this story more compelling and authentic. My husband, Ken, was the role model for Mr. Omar, and I know his memories of being a junior-high coach and club volleyball manager remain dear to him. I am beyond lucky to be surrounded by such a supportive family. Love, hugs, chocolate cake and Yorkshire pudding to you, you and you!